PEARL WHITE

LINDSAY MARIE MILLER

For my loving mother,

Thank you for bringing me into this world,

And challenging me to make the most of it.

~ ~

Preface

Eighteen. I had power now. Control over my life.

I could vote. I could purchase tobacco products—and even smoke them if I wanted.

I could get married.

But marriage was such a big thing. Wasn't it? I mean, if you're dating and the relationship ends, it's just a break-up. But when you're married, it's a divorce.

I looked down at the ring on my finger. It was beautiful. A white diamond.

Snow fell around me as I gazed up at the moon. I let out a long sigh. One that meant I'd been thinking a while—contemplating my future. Was there such a thing as destiny?

Tom had burdened me with a huge decision.

Why was I such a pessimist now? After everything that had happened, I should have been grateful—happy to be alive. Instead, near death had made me see the glass half empty. And I didn't know if there would ever be a time when it looked half full again.

I stood up and brushed the snow off my pants. As a Georgia girl, I'd never seen snow before. It was a phenomenon that had always fascinated me. Because it was scarce.

But here I was now, stepping through a bed of snow. I loved my winter wonderland. But nothing compared to the way I loved Tom.

He approached in the distance, and my stomach fluttered with excitement. I'd left him waiting with the biggest decision of his life. My life. Our life.

Separation wasn't an option. He had me until the day I died.

But I couldn't reconcile the implications. If I really did what he wanted me to.

The fear melted away when he asked me if I was cold. I nodded and he wrapped his arms around me. So I shut my eyes and buried my face in his chest. There may have been snow on the ground. But I was standing in a furnace of warmth.

That's when it hit me.

He was all I would ever need. He could shelter me through any storm. He already had.

Regardless, my question remained.

Was eighteen too young to get married?

Chapter 1

It was the day before my eighteenth birthday. And my parents actually wanted to celebrate.

I couldn't believe Eleanor had the decency to leave work early for a change. It had only taken her a couple years shy of two decades, but better late than never.

Even Jeffrey joined in on the celebration—he was the one to make reservations at an upscale Japanese restaurant in town. My friends were invited, but Eric and Jeanine weren't on speaking terms. So neither of them showed up. Which left the four of us.

Tom met us at the restaurant. He was waiting for me out front, hands in his pockets. I saw him from a distance in the parking lot, and a lucid smile tore across my face.

Dressed in blue jeans and a white button-down shirt, he looked good enough to eat. Despite our beach trip, Tom and I had yet to take things... further. It had been three months since I tossed the emerald necklace in the ocean. And that night had ended with me getting food poisoning. So sadly, it hadn't happened yet.

But I had my hopes up. Tom had promised me that tonight was the night.

"Hey, gorgeous." He pulled me into his arms and left a conservative kiss on my lips.

When I heard Eleanor's heels clicking in the distance, we straightened up. I kept my arm around him and leaned into his body. Then Tom held the door open for my parents.

"We've already made reservations," Eleanor said. "Thanks Tom."

"You're welcome," he said, keeping the door open for Jeffrey.

Jeffrey grinned and patted him on the back, crossing the threshold.

"Ready?" Tom nodded towards the restaurant.

I tilted my head up at him. "You have no idea."

He chuckled and followed me inside the restaurant.

After we'd been seated, I looked around the place to see if I recognized any familiar faces. Then I watched Jeffrey and Eleanor worrying over the menu. Since they were distracted, I slipped my hand beneath the table and laced my fingers through Tom's.

He kept his eyes on his menu, but squeezed

my hand back. We were at a booth, so holding hands in secret was easy to do. I was blushing already, just thinking about tonight.

"What are you thinking about getting, Addie?" Eleanor asked.

"Umm..." I looked at the menu for the first time. "I'm not sure."

"Why don't we order some appetizers?" Jeffrey suggested.

Eleanor agreed. So when the waitress came by, Jeffrey ordered a plate of wontons and egg rolls. Everyone else knew what they wanted, so I chose the same main course as Tom. I hardly paid attention to what it was. I felt too nervous and excited for food right now.

"I can't believe you're turning eighteen tomorrow," Eleanor said.

She was leaving to go out of town in the morning. Which was the only reason we were celebrating my birthday tonight. Regardless, it was more effort than she usually put in.

"Yeah." Jeffrey took a sip of his ice water. "Time really does fly."

I forced a smile as Tom cradled my hand. "Where is Jimmy?"

"Oh, I'm sorry." Eleanor frowned. "He couldn't make it tonight, honey."

"That's okay." I saw a noticeable change in Jeffrey when I brought my real father up. For years, I'd thought they were my biological parents. But the truth is—my mother had died many years ago. Jimmy was my true father, my birth dad. And I loved him.

"So how is the college search going?" Eleanor asked. "Are you planning any more visits soon?"

Tom and I had been visiting colleges together. But I knew her reason for bringing up the future. It was a ploy to change the subject. And protect her husband's feelings.

"Uhh." Tom looked at me. "I'm not sure."

"I heard Georgia Tech was after you," Jeffrey said. "It's a great school."

"Thanks, Mr. Smith." Tom locked his fingers with mine. This time, they were above the table. So everyone could see that we were holding hands. "But I don't think it's the right fit for me."

"Why not?" Jeffrey badgered. "Do you know how low their acceptance rate is?"

"Yeah." Tom nodded. "I mean, yes sir. I know."

"Addie, what about you?" Eleanor stared at me. "Have you given any more thought to SCAD? I know it's a fortune, but it is prestigious. And Jimmy is there."

Jeffrey bowed his head. Talking about my real father was hurting him.

"Well." I looked at Tom. "I don't think it's the right fit for me."

"Why not?" Eleanor asked. "For the past two months, all you've done is work on your portfolio. I know I haven't been great about supporting your art in the past. But—"

6

"Actually, Mrs. Smith, we've applied to Georgia," Tom revealed.

"Oh." Eleanor's brow shot to the ceiling. "Georgia."

"Yes ma'am." He draped his arm over my shoulders with a smile.

"I'm not the right fit for Georgia Tech," I explained. "And SCAD is only for art students. So..." I drifted off, distracted by the mere presence of Tom.

"So, we've decided to apply somewhere with more diversity," he said.

Eleanor looked puzzled. And Jeffrey, well, he was still wounded from earlier. I'd have to find a way to keep Jimmy's name from coming up around Jeffrey. It was really starting to bother him.

"More diversity?" Eleanor asked. "But Addie, what about SCAD?"

"And Tom," Jeffrey jumped in. "I don't want to tell you what to do but—"

"I get it, Mr. Smith. Georgia Tech is a great school. I understand."

"Then what's the problem?" Jeffrey stared at Tom.

"Georgia Tech is in Atlanta," I said.

"And SCAD is here," Tom said—echoing a similar sentiment.

Eleanor fluttered her dark lashes. "I'm not following."

"We want to be together." I looked each of them in the eye.

"We've talked about it," Tom said. "And we decided that it's more important for us to be together."

"Yeah, if we go to Georgia, we'll both be in Athens," I added. "And we can both major in what we want. They've got plenty of programs for the arts and the sciences."

"I see." Eleanor chewed on a piece of ice. Then the waitress came with our food, and everyone was quiet until she left. There was a thick layer of tension at our table.

I was surprised.

"Addie, I didn't realize that the two of you were so serious," Jeffrey said.

"Well, we are." I shrugged my shoulders.

It had been almost a year since we'd met. If Jeffrey and Eleanor couldn't see how we felt about each other, that wasn't my problem. They were the ones who left all the time. The ones who were never around.

Our relationship had unfolded before their very eyes.

They just hadn't been here to witness it.

"I care about your daughter," Tom said. "And we are as serious as it gets."

Jeffrey ordered a bottle of wine for the table, and my bubble burst.

"I thought you'd be happy for me," I sighed. "For us."

It wasn't like I needed their approval. I could live without it. But it would have been nice to finally have them participate in something. They'd been absent for so long.

"I never said I wasn't happy about it," Jeffrey said.

"Well, you sure don't act like it. Neither of you do."

"Addie, your father and I just want to make sure you're making the right decision for you. I mean, I didn't meet your father until I was much older. You can't plan your whole life around someone else. Because if it doesn't work out..."

"This is the right decision for me," I snapped. "This is what I want."

"I think sometimes you forget that you're very young," Eleanor said.

"And I think sometimes you forget that you haven't been around my whole life," I hissed. "Tom has. He's protected me and looked out for me when no one else would."

Silence fell over the table like rain in a storm.

"You know what?" Tears burned the back of my eyes. "I don't even want to be here."

I grabbed my purse and got out of the booth. Because of the way we were sitting, Tom had to get out with me. It was the only way for me to get close to the door.

"Addie, wait." Jeffrey said. "Don't leave. We haven't even ordered dessert."

I looked at Tom. And he saw the tears in my eyes.

"Take me home," I whispered. "Please."

Tom left cash on the table for the tip. Then he nodded at them. "Sorry."

When he turned around, I was already waiting for him by the door. He led me out to his car and opened the door before I got in. Then he walked around the other side and climbed in, starting the car so we could get the hell out of here.

I burst into tears the minute he pulled away. If it had been anyone but Tom, I would have been humiliated. But he was the one person I could be truly vulnerable around.

"I just wanted them to be happy for me," I sobbed. "Would that kill them?"

Tom kept his eyes on the road.

"I mean, is it too much to ask? That I just want them to accept whatever I choose? I just want them to approve. For once in my life, can't they just say I'm on the right track?"

"I'm sure they just want what they think is best for you," Tom said.

"What they think is best for me?" I glared. "They don't care what's best for me!"

"You don't know that." His knuckles turned white over the steering wheel.

"Well, I do." I looked out the window. "I've known it for years now."

"Where do you want me to take you?" he asked.

"Home," I murmured. "With you."

He stopped at a red light and rubbed my back. "Come here."

So I leaned across the console and wrapped my arms around him. As always, he was such a comfort to me. Strong. Warm. A real man trapped in a teenager's body.

He drove the rest of the way home with my head on his chest.

* * *

I fell asleep in the car. Tom tried to wake me up, but I was irritable and groggy. Even in my sleep, I couldn't forget what Jeffrey and Eleanor had said. Their words stung.

Tom pulled his Mustang into the garage and then carried me into the mansion in his arms. I had no energy, because I hadn't slept a wink the night before. I'd been thinking about what Tom and I had planned for tonight.

It was late October in Savannah, but the temperature had been dropping every week. The weather channel was predicting a record winter for the area. The coldest in history.

Tom laid me down on the couch and started a fire. Then he covered my body with a warm blanket. It was cozy and soft, so I snuggled beneath the fabric and yawned.

When I opened my eyes, Tom was pulling my feet into his lap. I had socks on, but my toes were still frozen. I'd always had cold feet. But they were arctic tonight.

"Always so cold." Tom took my socks off and rubbed the soles of my feet.

"Do you think we're crazy?" I asked. "For

being so serious, so young."

"Addie, if you're having second thoughts about Georgia—"

"I'm not." I sat up and knelt down on the couch. "I want to be with you."

He cupped my cheek in his hand. "I want to be with you, too."

Liking that answer, I leaned in and put my mouth on his. Tom groaned as our lips touched, circling his arms around my back. I sat down in his lap and ran my fingers through his hair. My body knew what it wanted. Tonight had been a long time coming.

"Hey." Tom pulled back. "Do you want to watch a movie?"

I gave him a funny look.

"It's not your birthday yet."

I narrowed my eyes and got out of his lap. "Fine."

Tom approached the entertainment unit by the fire place. But I sulked on the couch and crossed my arms over my chest. When he looked back at me, my skin was on fire.

"What do you want to watch?" He opened the cabinet of DVDs.

I dragged myself off the couch and swayed beside him. "Something funny."

He looked at the movies while I curled my arms around his waist.

"Will Ferrell," I suggested. "I want someone to make me laugh."

"Okay." Tom grinned. "Anchorman or Kicking and Screaming?"

"Kicking and Screaming," I nibbled at his ear. "Because that's what you're going to be doing tonight."

His eyes looked like they were about to pop out of his head.

"I'm just kidding," I giggled.

"Funny." He popped the DVD in and grabbed the remote.

I bit my lip and sauntered to the couch. There was a flat screen TV hanging over the fireplace. But we hardly ever used it. When I had him to myself, the last thing I wanted to do was watch a movie. Except for tonight, when he was being ridiculous and stubborn.

Impatient, I drummed my fingers and looked at the clock on the wall. It was only a matter of time before I got what I wanted. With a countdown in mind, I could get through the rest of the night. As long as he held up his end of the bargain.

Kicking and Screaming was hilarious. Despite being impatient, I was glad we watched a movie together. After dinner with Jeffrey and Eleanor, I needed a reason to laugh.

"Do you want to see your cake?" Tom asked. He turned the TV off and put the remote up.

"You made me a cake?" I swooned. He must have seen the stars in my eyes.

"Yeah." He grabbed my hand and led me into

the kitchen.

There was a chocolate birthday cake on the table. As he pulled me closer, I looked over his shoulder and my mouth fell open. It was decorated in maroon icing.

HAPPY BIRTHDAY ADDIE

Maybe it wasn't that big of a deal. But that homemade cake meant the world to me.

I leaned into his back, because the full weight of my body couldn't take it. Tears stung my eyes. When I lifted my hand to wipe one away, Tom squeezed my waist.

"Hey," he crooned. "What's wrong?"

"No one's ever gotten me a cake before."

He blinked. "For your birthday?"

"No." I looked at the cake. "Never."

He caressed my cheek and nestled his fingers in my hair. "Addie."

"Eleanor isn't so big on celebrating birthdays."

"But what about tonight? We went out to dinner," he said.

"Yeah. That's because you were there."

As a kid, Eleanor had shown little interest in raising me. Jeffrey had a better aptitude for parenting. But he was so flaky and aloof that it didn't really matter.

It wasn't like we'd never celebrated my birthday before. But once I was too old to go trick or treating, the annual tradition of turning a year older stopped as well. Eleanor wasn't big on gift giving, even at Christmas time. So I knew not to expect any kind of present.

Tom pulled me into a hug and kissed my hair. "I promise I'll take care of you."

I nuzzled his chest and admired the cake he'd made for me.

"I better put this in the fridge." He covered the cake. "I barely had enough time to ice it before I left to meet y'all for dinner."

Tom put the cake in the fridge and shut the door.

"Why did you start watching me?" I asked.

He froze.

I walked up behind him. "Was it because you liked me or—"

"That was a long time ago, Addie." He turned around. "We were just kids."

"I know, but..." I looked into his eyes, unable to find the words.

"I liked you. Okay?" He lifted my chin. "It's not like I'm some stalker."

"I never said you were. But why did you like me?"

He pursed his lips with a deep breath. "Because I thought you were beautiful."

I couldn't breathe. Everything felt tingly, dizzy. I opened my mouth. But no words came out. There was no way to describe what I was feeling. What I'd always felt for him.

"I think you're pretty beautiful, too." I slipped my hand beneath his shirt sleeve.

His pupils dilated. He stood up straight. He

clenched his jaw.

"I love the cake." I put my hand on his chest.

He smiled, peering down at me. "You haven't even tasted it yet."

"It doesn't matter." I touched the back of his neck. "I already know I'm going to want more."

Tom took my hand off his chest and held it instead. "Let's not get the cart before the horse."

"When do I get to see my present?" I moved until our torsos were flush.

He rocked back on his heels with a growl. "Come with me."

There were so many emotions racing through my head all at once.

As he led me to the staircase, I thought about the life we'd shared so far. And the one we would build together. I saw a future with marriage and kids. A house of our own.

But when I walked into his bedroom, Tom made me sit down on the bed. Then he got out his guitar and pulled up a chair. I crossed my legs and waited, pulsing with anticipation.

"I wanted to play you something. Is that okay?" he asked.

"Of course." I glanced at the clock. It was ten p.m. Only a couple hours to go.

He plucked the strings for a few measures. I recognized the melody, and he laughed. It was "Happy Birthday to You" — a simple and timeless song, no doubt.

But there was something special about Tom

playing it for me.

I clapped my hands when he was finished. But then Tom just kept playing. They were all covers — better heard acoustically. The Police. Coldplay. John Mayer. Ed Sheeran.

When he sang, I felt all mushy inside. Butterflies battled it out in my stomach. And there was sweat on my palms. As I checked the clock, my heart pounded something fierce.

11:40

Only twenty minutes to go.

I ran my hands over my jeans. As much as I wanted this, I had no idea how nervous I was going to get. Was I excited? Yes. But I also kind of felt like throwing up.

"I know it's getting late," Tom said. "But I just wanted to play you one more."

"Okay." I nodded. There was a tightening sensation in my chest.

He strummed a sweet melody with his eyes closed. It took me a while to recognize the song. And then a few measures more for me to realize that I'd never heard it before.

His voice was breathy tonight. Sultry. Sensual. Seductive.

It's a well-known fact that chicks dig dudes who play guitar. I don't know that I'd word it like that, but you get the point. He was serenading me. And I was one of those chicks.

When he sang the last note, there were tears in my eyes. He set the guitar aside and got down on his knees, folding his fingers through mine. And I trembled from his touch.

"You wrote me a song," I whispered.

"Yeah. I did." He gave me a sexy grin. "Did you like it?"

I nodded. Then I put my hands on his face and kissed him.

"Why are you crying?" He rubbed his nose against mine.

"You really love me. Don't you?"

"Yes." He pressed a kiss to my cheek. "I always have."

I tugged at the collar of his shirt until his mouth landed on mine. Then I twisted my fingers through his hair and curled my legs around his waist. He trailed a line of kisses down my neck, and my head dipped back to give him easier access.

Everything was so loud. His breath in my ear. My booming heart.

My skin crawled with need and desire. He pushed me onto his bed, and I wrapped my arms around his back. As his lips swept across my collar bone, I leaned back and relaxed.

"Take off your shirt," I gasped.

He sat up on his knees, while I tore through the buttons. Then he let me push the sleeves down his muscled-up arms. His skin was still tan — leftover from the summer.

I dropped his shirt on the floor. And his golden eyes pierced straight through me like a dagger to the heart. He took my hand and put it over his chest. He felt warm.

"Are you sure you want to do this?" he asked.

"Yes." I kissed his left pec. "I'm sure."

He weaved his fingers through my hair and cradled the back of my head. Then he kissed me until we were lying down again. I ran my fingertips down his back, tracing every dip and shallow in his exquisite body. And his hand slipped beneath my shirt.

Eager to help, I lifted my arms in the air. "Take it off."

He chuckled at my zeal. Until my elbow slammed into his head.

"Ow," he winced, retracting from me.

"Tom, I'm so sorry." I touched his arm. "Are you okay?"

"Yeah." He rubbed the spot where I'd hit him.

"Where does it hurt?" I asked. "Show me. I'll kiss it better."

Tom pointed, and I kissed his hair. "How's that?"

"Much better." He cupped my cheek in his hand.

I put my arms up in the air. "I won't move this time. I promise."

He kissed my neck and then pulled my shirt over my head.

Impatient, I crawled closer and got in his lap. Then we were kissing again. And his hands slithered down my spine. I dug my nails into his back and savored every kiss.

An alarm went off in his room. I looked at the clock on his nightstand.

It was glaring red.

12:00

It was midnight on October 23rd. My birthday.

Tom reached around me to silence the alarm. I didn't think twice about it — why his alarm was set for midnight in the first place. I was too distracted.

I rubbed his shoulders and cocked my head to the side. "Aren't you going to wish me happy birthday?"

Tom uncoiled my legs from his waist. "Happy Birthday."

He got out of bed and put his shirt back on.

"What are you doing?" I furrowed my brow, confused and hurt.

"It's your birthday." He fastened the buttons on his shirt.

"Yeah, I know." I pushed the covers back and stood up.

"So that means you're eighteen now." He picked my shirt up off the floor and handed it to me.

"Umm, isn't that kind of implied?" I put my hands on my hips.

"You're eighteen. I'm seventeen."

"Duh." I threw my shirt on the ground. "What does that have to do with anything?"

"It means that we can't have sex until my

eighteenth birthday. Unless you want to get arrested." He walked out of the room, while I stood there gaping after him.

"Tom!" I followed him down the stairs. "You made me a promise."

He stopped on the last step. Then he turned around and unbuttoned his shirt. "Put this on."

"I don't want to!" I stomped my foot like a toddler.

Tom forced my arms through the sleeves and fastened the middle three buttons.

"Why are you doing this?" I felt like crying. "Why are you teasing me?"

Tom traced my lower lip with his thumb. "I never meant to tease you."

"Well, I hardly think what we were about to do constitutes statutory rape."

He sighed and traced his knuckles down my throat.

"You really think somebody is going to have me arrested for sleeping with you?" I shook my head at him. "I feel like you tricked me! On my birthday!"

I brushed past him and paced in the den.

"You knew I was turning eighteen tonight! Why did you lie to me?"

"I never lied," he said.

"You promised me that tonight we were going to—" I spun around and gasped.

He was down on one knee with a box in his hand. "There is another way."

I put my hand over my mouth. He opened the box. There was a ring inside.

"If we were married, you could love me anytime you want."

I wanted to laugh, because it was so absurd.

"Tom. I'm eighteen. We're not even done with high school yet."

"If we were married, no laws would be broken."

I shook my head and chewed my lip.

"If we were married, you would really be mine."

"I don't understand. All this, just so we can have sex?" I questioned.

"Maybe I want more from you than just sex," he said.

I looked at the ring. It was at least a carat.

"It was your grandmother's," he said. "Grandpa gave it to me before he..."

There was a white diamond in the center with tiny emeralds around the band.

"I don't get it. What about high school? College? We haven't even—"

"I want to marry you. You know you're gonna end up with me. Why wait?"

It was stupid. It was impulsive. It was romantic.

So I said yes.

"Yes?" he asked.

"Yes." I nodded, melting into a blubbery mess.

Tom slid the ring on my finger, and I was shaking. When he stood up, I molded into his perfect body and wilted under his touch. He kissed me again and again.

I was speechless.

He wrapped me in his arms, as I eyed the ring on my finger.

I was ten minutes into my eighteenth birthday.

And we were engaged.

Chapter 2

It felt weird on my hand. Almost like it weighed me down somehow.

I took the ring off my finger when I was getting ready for school. I had to be there early for a club meeting, so Tom and I drove separately. For that, I was relieved.

We had fewer classes together this year. Maybe it was because we were seniors. Tom had more electives than me, since he'd received so many credits when he was homeschooled. Regardless, we had a couple AP courses together. And that was enough.

Especially since I'd been hiding from him before the sun came up today.

"Happy Birthday!" Eric caught me at my locker between classes.

"Hey!" I patted his back when he gave me a hug. "Thank you."

"Here." He handed me a package. It was wrapped in blue paper.

"Eric, you didn't have to get me anything." I blushed.

"No, I wanted to," he nudged. "Open it."

Smiling up at him, I tore through the paper and lifted the lid on a brown box. There was tissue paper inside. And a University of Georgia sweatshirt with the team mascot on the front.

"Uga." I sing-songed. I loved that bulldog. He was just so cute.

"I know you haven't gotten in yet," he said. "I thought it would be good luck."

"Thank you, Eric." I gave him a hug. "I love it."

"Well, I'm glad." He leaned against the lockers. "So have you talked to Jeanine lately?"

"Yeah." I shoved a couple books in my locker. "But I'm guessing you haven't?"

"What am I supposed to do?" he asked. "She hates my guts." He looked over his shoulder. "Just like everyone else at this school."

"We don't all hate your guts." I looked at him. "Why don't you just call her?"

"She won't talk to me!" He clung to his backpack strap. "But I don't blame her."

"Eric, we all know what happened that night. You didn't do anything wrong."

"Yeah? Well then why does it feel like I'm a criminal or something?"

"Happy Birthday!" Jeanine snuck up behind

me and tapped my shoulder.

"Thank you!" I turned around and she saw Eric standing beside me.

"Oh." She looked like she wanted to run and hide.

"I'll go." Eric touched my arm. "Happy Birthday, Addie."

Jeanine watched him walk away, while I sighed. "What's that?"

There was a purple gift bag in her hand. "This is for you."

I opened the gift, but her thoughts were elsewhere. I caught her looking back over her shoulder at Eric. Students darted out of the way when he walked by, ostracizing him.

"Wow." I pulled a green sweater out of the bag. "Jeanine, this is gorgeous!"

"It's cashmere." She touched the fabric. "Very expensive."

"You didn't have to do that — spend all that money on me."

"Yes, I did." She gave me a hug. "You're the only one around here who will put up with me."

I put the sweater in the gift bag and stowed it away in my locker.

"Is that what Eric got you?" She eyed the Georgia bulldogs sweatshirt.

"Yeah." I slipped it into the gift bag. "I guess the two of you kind of think alike."

She rolled her eyes with a long-suffering sigh.

"Are you ever going to talk to him again?" I

asked.

She leaned against the locker beside mine, watching students walk by.

"You've got to get over this. He was just asking about you."

"He was?" She perked up.

"Yeah. I can tell he misses you. I know you miss him, too."

"Whatever." She pushed off the lockers. "I've got to get to class."

"You can't ignore him forever!" I yelled after her.

She waved a hand in the air, but her back was turned. Tom passed her in the hallway as she headed to class. When he saw me, I shut my locker and clicked the lock in place.

"Hey." His hand settled on my waist. "I missed you."

I braided my fingers behind his neck and tingled when he kissed me.

"What did Jeanine say?" He supported my back with his hands.

"Oh, she was just wishing me a happy birthday. And she got me a sweater."

"No, I mean, what did she say about us?" He held me with the look in his eyes.

"Umm." I looked down the hall. "Nothing."

"You didn't tell her?" He grabbed my hand, and his face fell.

"Tom." I pulled my hand back and tucked it under my arm.

"Where's your ring?" He put his hand on my locker, caging me in.

"I left it at home."

He groaned and looked away, placing his hands on his hips.

"Are we engaged or not?" he demanded.

"What?" The bell rang. "Of course we are."

"Then why are you keeping it a secret from everyone?" he asked.

We were arguing in an empty hallway. Which meant I was really late for class.

"I'm not! It's just..." I hesitated. "Do we have to talk about this now?"

"It's just what? Finish your sentence."

"Who gets married at eighteen? What will everyone think?"

Hurt flashed across his face. "I thought we didn't care what they think."

"We don't, but everyone is gonna start saying I'm pregnant or something."

"Well." He took a step back. "We know that's impossible."

"Tom, I'm gonna start wearing it, I promise."

"When?" he asked.

"I don't know." I threw my hands in the air. "I haven't even told my parents yet."

"Jimmy knows."

"What?" I snapped. "You told him? Without even asking me first?"

"I asked his permission for your hand in marriage. Excuse me for being a gentleman."

He left me standing there at my locker. I watched him walk away and flinched when the double doors slammed behind him. This was too much. Way too much.

Turning eighteen was more than I'd signed up for.

* * *

After school, I drove across town to the Savannah College of Art and Design. I had plans with Jimmy to celebrate my birthday. The moment I walked in his office, I was assaulted by an army of balloons. The biggest one screamed HAPPY BIRTHDAY!

"What did you do? Raid every store in town?" I pushed my way through the balloons.

"It's the first birthday I get to celebrate with my daughter," he said.

"Well, eighteen isn't all that it's cracked up to be." I took a seat in front of his desk.

Jimmy shut the door and dragged most of the balloons to the corner of the room. "Where's Tom?"

"We had a fight." I checked my nail beds. Even though I wasn't a manicure kind of girl.

"On your birthday?" He leaned against the edge of his desk.

"About my birthday." I looked into his brown eyes and sulked.

"Let me guess. Is this about him proposing?" he asked.

"I can't believe you knew! Why would he tell

you without asking me?"

"You've never heard of a guy getting the father's permission first?" he wondered.

"Well, I've never really had a father." I gazed at him. "Until you."

"So... did you tell him no?" He crossed his ankles

"No!" I felt so bratty for complaining. "I told him yes."

He looked like he wasn't buying it. "Where's the ring?"

"Is that all you men ever think about?" I stood up and lingered near the door.

"What's going on, kid?"

"I'm not wearing it because—" I met his gaze and sat back down. He was amused. "Well. What is everyone going to think? Engaged at eighteen? I mean—"

"Most of them will probably think you're pregnant. The rest will just think you're crazy."

"Wow. Thanks, Jimmy. That's really helpful."

He chuckled. "I don't know what you're complaining about. That boy loves you."

That shut me up right there. "You know it, too?"

"I knew it the first time I saw you two together. He's crazy about you."

"How would you know?" I leaned forward in the chair.

"Because I felt the same way about your mother."

Now I felt like a jerk. "I'm sorry."

"I'm done teaching for the day. Let me take you to lunch."

"It's almost four o' clock," I noted.

"So?" He stood up and grabbed his jacket. "It's your birthday."

I smiled and rocked back on my heels. Jimmy led me out the door as we made our way to the parking lot. While he talked, I wondered what it would be like to attend college here. For so long, I'd been living without a father. Maybe Eleanor was right.

If I stayed in Savannah, I could pursue my dreams right here—at a college tailored for artists. After seventeen years without him, it would be nice to see Jimmy anytime I wanted. The move to Athens would mean I'd rarely get to visit more than a few times a year.

We had lunch at a local bar and grill. Even though I'd been against the idea, I'd hardly eaten today. Since last night, a great big knot had developed in my stomach. I was scared.

"So let me get this straight." Jimmy cradled a glass of iced tea. "Your sweet doting boyfriend got down on his knee and asked you to marry him and you're pissed?"

"Well." I looked at the fries on my plate. "When you put it like that—"

"Listen, kid, in some respect I get it. You're young, vulnerable, scared. But you'd know by now if he were too good to be true. And I don't think he is."

"It's just that we went out to dinner last night and—well—Jeffrey and Eleanor didn't seem too pleased. I know they're just my adoptive parents. It's not like with you."

There was a twinkle in his eye.

"But they don't support my relationship with Tom or the fact that we're choosing to go to the same college. After all these years, it would be nice for them to just accept me."

Jimmy leaned back in his chair. "Was this a birthday dinner?"

"Yeah." I furrowed my brow. "Eleanor said you couldn't make it."

He snickered. "Yeah, it's real hard for me to show up when I'm not invited."

Flames ripped across my skin. "She told me she asked you to come. And that you said you couldn't make it. I knew I should have just called you myself! That is so like her!"

"It's okay." He raised his hand — a signal for me to calm down.

"No, it's not." I shook my head. "My whole life they've been anything but good parents. I'm tired of playing their game. It's my life. I don't belong to them. I never did."

"If you want my advice, you need to spend less time worrying about them and more time focusing on Tom. The poor guy's never really had a family. And now—"

"I'm all he has."

"It's more than that, Addie. That boy would break his neck to see you happy."

I blushed at such a fond opinion of Tom. "He's not really a boy."

"He's seventeen."

"He's more of a man than any teenager I've ever met," I said.

"Then what's the problem?" he asked. "It's your birthday. He wants to marry you. Shouldn't you be jumping up and down?"

"I always thought we'd end up together. I just didn't think marriage would be on the agenda before high school graduation."

"Do you want to marry Tom?" Jimmy looked me right in the eye.

"Yes." My cheek twitched at the thought.

"Men are usually more practical. Maybe he's just planning ahead. If you get married now, you could move in with him. Then when you go off to college, the two of you will already be used to living together. It might make things easier for the future."

"I guess I never thought about it like that."

It was true. Tom always planned ahead. Maybe he was thinking of our future.

"But we're just so young." It was the point I kept coming back to.

"You just got engaged last night," he said. "It's not like you're getting married tomorrow."

"You're right." To be honest, I hadn't considered a long engagement.

"Who says you have to get married the minute you get engaged?" Jimmy chewed on a piece of ice. "I think you're reading this all wrong."

"I think I am, too."

"Maybe Tom is old-fashioned, but do you prefer the alternative? Nowadays, most guys want to date about ten years and won't even consider marriage until they're thirty-five."

I laughed. "Now that you mention it, that sounds much worse."

At that rate, we would have been dating almost twenty years before the wedding.

"When he proposed, I guess I just wasn't expecting it. That's all," I said.

"You're shell-shocked. I get it. But after everything the two of you have been through, can you blame him?" Jimmy asked.

He had made quite a few good points. But I'd never thought about that—carpe diem. We'd come close to death so many times. And we hadn't even lived yet. No wonder Tom was in a hurry to make sure we didn't miss anything. Life is short enough as it is.

"The thought of losing him..." I drifted off. "I couldn't bear it."

"And what if he feels the same way about you?" he asked.

I felt like a fool. Tom was prepared to start our life together now. By now, I should have learned that neither of us could predict what lay around the bend.

I'd wanted him to love me. But Tom wanted more than that. He wanted marriage and commitment. A true proclamation of our love for each other.

He wanted me to be his wife. Because he knew a time might come when he wouldn't be able to ask me. We'd already witnessed it first hand — the danger of loving each other. And I'd be damned if we missed out on the best part.

"You're really smart," I told Jimmy.

"Just trying to help you see his side."

I twirled the straw around in my drink. "You like Tom. Don't you?"

"Yeah. Why wouldn't I? He's the man who loves my daughter."

* * *

It was dark when I reached the mansion. I'd driven home and left my car in the drive. Then scampered through the thickets of the forest — like we used to.

I found Tom sitting alone by the fire. There was sadness in his eyes as he watched the flames. I leaned into the doorway and crossed my arms over my chest.

It was a rare sight to behold. My handsome beau lost without me.

When I showed myself, he lifted his head in surprise. I got down on my knees and caressed his face. He kept his eyes on me, almost like he was afraid to look away.

I kissed him. Softly at first. And he was a loyal

subject — responding to my touch.

His hands slithered down my back as he curled his arms around me. I ran my fingers through his hair and sighed, tingling all over. Soon we were chest to chest, and he pulled me into his lap. I knelt down on the couch and cupped the back of his neck in my hands.

"I love you," I whispered. "And I want to marry you."

Tom gasped for breath and leaned his forehead against mine.

"I'm sorry about before." I stroked the stubble on his jaw. "I don't know what I was thinking."

He smiled and circled his thumb over my cheek. Then he kissed me tenderly. And I knew he was stopping things before they went too far. It made me feel like a masochist.

I put my hand on his chest, and he glanced down. "You're wearing your ring."

I nodded, a hint of rosy blush staining my cheeks. "I love it, Tom. It's perfect."

He touched the small of my back and gifted another kiss. "You had me worried there."

"I'm sorry." I looked at the ring. "I guess the idea of marriage kind of freaked me out. But I never imagined I'd be getting engaged so young."

"Does it really matter how old we are? Or what everyone will think?" he asked.

"No." I lifted his chin. "I want everyone to know that you belong to me."

He chuckled. "Oh. Do you now? I thought it

was the other way around?"

Pressing out a small smile, I rubbed his neck. "Your mine and I'm yours."

"Sounds good to me." He kissed me again and then buried his face in my neck. I put my head on his shoulder and closed my eyes, touching his back. We held each other like that until I drifted off in his arms. But then he woke me up and saw my crabby side.

"What?" I whined, nuzzling his chest.

"Your birthday's not over yet." He kissed my cheek. "Wake up. I want to show you something."

"Can't you just show me in the morning?" I was comfortable and warm. I didn't want to move.

"Nope." He got off the couch while I grumbled. "Get up, birthday girl."

Rolling my eyes, I stood up and leaned into his body. "Fine. What is it?"

He laughed when I put all of my weight on him. "Do you want me to carry you?"

If he was offering, I sure wasn't going to turn him down. "Okay."

So he tucked his arm beneath my knees and lifted me in the air. I put my head on his chest and curled my arms around his neck. In that moment, my life felt like a fairy tale.

He was the man of my dreams. And he was— quite literally—sweeping me off my feet.

I closed my eyes as he carried me upstairs. I thought he might take me to his bedroom and serenade me with another song. But he passed his room and kept walking, as my heart fluttered with intrigue.

He toted me down a long corridor with doors on either side. I'd often wondered who had lived here in generations past. Someone must have had a lot of children, because I couldn't see any other reason for so many bedrooms. The upkeep on this place must have been taxing.

Tom set me on my feet in front of a white door. "Close your eyes."

"Why?" I grinned, on the edge of my seat. "What's in there?"

"Come on, Addie. Please?"

I looked at him and the door.

"I spent a lot of time on this," he griped.

"Fine." I shut my eyes. "They're closed."

I reached for Tom's arm when I lost my balance. Without sight, my sense of hearing was heightened. So I heard him unlock the door, and the tiny squeak that followed when he opened it.

He got behind me and put his hands over my eyes.

"Tom, they're already closed!" I felt even more off balance now.

"Well, how else can I stop you from peeking?"

I reached for something to grab on to as he led me into the room. But that was no use, so I held on to his arms instead. He steered me towards the center and then told me to stay still. I put my hands over my eyes when he pulled away, so he couldn't accuse me of peeking. Then I swayed backwards and nearly crashed into a wall until he grabbed me.

"I was planning on showing this to you in the daylight, but it's too late for that now."

"Tom, I'm sure I'll love it no matter what," I insisted. Not only was I dying to see this, he'd kept me in suspense so long that I couldn't take it anymore.

"All right. Wait." He turned me to the right. "Okay. Open your eyes."

I lowered my hands and stared at the wall in front of me. Paintings hung from left to right. Beautiful landscapes of places I'd never seen before. A tropical rainforest. A deserted island. Rolling hills. Frozen rivers. English castles and Scottish moors.

"Tom, these are beautiful." I took the time to study each one.

He tugged at my hand. "There's more."

I turned around and saw more artwork hanging on the opposite wall.

My art. Daniel's art. All the paintings Jimmy had given us last summer.

There was an easel and canvas by the window. The same one I'd accepted when Daniel was alive. It drew me in like a magnet, as I discovered a plethora of art supplies.

It was a room of my very own — explicitly for my greatest passion, apart from Tom.

"We chose this room because of the view." Tom opened the French doors. "No one is ever going to use this balcony." He went on talking, but I was mesmerized.

Antoinette's portrait was hanging on the wall by the French doors.

"Are you coming?" Tom looked back at me.

I followed him onto the balcony and looked out.

"There is plenty of room for you to paint. And the view's not too shabby."

"Yeah." I shivered and put my hands on the railing. It was so beautiful up here. I could see the moonlight and the trees. The vast darkness of the forest. It was enchanting.

"Do you like it?" He gazed into my eyes.

"To be honest, I don't know what to say."

His face fell, as he bit his lip and leaned against the railing. I put my hand on his chest and searched his eyes. But he was looking down, thinking he had disappointed me.

"Why did you do all this?" I asked.

"Because I want you to feel like you have a home. Here with me."

"I do feel at home with you." I grazed his cheek. "I never have with anyone else."

We kissed beneath the stars as he wrapped his arms around me.

"I love it," I said. "It's too much really. You shouldn't have—"

He put a finger to my lips. "Don't start with me now."

"How did you do all this? Pull it off without

me knowing?"

"I had a little help from your father. He pitched in too with the new paintings."

So it was a joint birthday present from Jimmy and Tom. My two favorite people.

"You really believe in me, don't you?" I asked.

Tom cupped my cold cheek in his warm hand. "I do."

He turned me around in his arms so my back was against his chest. Together, we looked out at the land. Acres of virgin timber that belonged to no one but us. At eighteen, it was a strange feeling to have.

"So I was thinking." Tom put his chin on my shoulder and circled his arms around my waist. "Maybe one day we could put in a pool. It gets so hot in the summer. It would be nice for the kids."

"Kids?" I looked back at him.

"Yeah." He nodded. "Maybe four or five."

"Four or five?" I shouted. "You remember I'm the one who has to have them?"

"I know." He put his hand on my stomach. "And I can't wait to make them."

"You do realize that you're like thirty-five, right," I teased.

"Actually, now that I think about it, thirty-two sounds like a better fit."

I looked up at him and laughed, filled to the brim with happiness. Everything guys are afraid of? Well, Tom was simply immune. Sometimes, I thought it was a bad thing. Because it even freaked me out. But it showed me just how strong his love was.

"You've given me the best birthday a girl could ask for," I said.

He kissed my cheek and whispered, "You just wait until our wedding night."

He left me gaping on the balcony, while I watched him go inside. When he turned back, my cheeks were scalding with blush. I followed him and took his hand.

"Is that a promise?" I leaned my head back to look up at him.

"Mm-hmm." He cradled my face in his hands, brushing his lips against mine.

I felt sated and sleepy, drunk on love. Big dreams. Big plans. Our future.

We went downstairs and Tom lit my birthday cake. I blew out the candles and made a wish. He leaned across the table and kissed me, smearing chocolate icing on my face.

I was eighteen now, and it felt like my dreams had already come true.

Chapter 3

You're engaged?!?" Jeanine squealed. "Oh my god!"

"Shh." I glared at her. "Keep it down."

"Let me see the ring."

I showed her my hand and her eyes lit up. "Addie, that thing is huge."

"It was my grandmother's," I said.

"So how did it happen? How did he propose? Have you set a date yet?"

I took a breath. "He surprised me the night before my birthday."

"Oh, that is so romantic!"

"Yeah, I definitely didn't see it coming." I looked at the ring on my finger.

"So when's the wedding?" She was so eager. "I'm invited right?"

"Of course you are. But I'm not really sure about all the details yet."

"Oh my god! This is so exciting. I can't believe it! You're getting married!"

So much for keeping it down.

"Who's getting married?" Eric strolled up, much to Jeanine's dismay.

"I am," I answered.

Eric stood stock-still, his blue eyes glazing over the rock. "Why?"

"Wow, that's supportive. Leave it to you to ruin the mood." Jeanine shoved his shoulder and brushed past him, walking off. I was surprised she'd stuck around for as long as she did. It might be a new millennium before she welcomed him into her life again.

"Sorry." Eric shook his head, watching her go. "I didn't mean it like that."

"I know it may come as a surprise." I grabbed a text book from my locker. "But we really love each other. I've always known it was him — that he was the one. With everything that's happened, we figure, why wait? You never know when it's your last tomorrow."

"That's awfully poetic of you," Eric said. He leaned back as students passed him by, pausing long enough to glare before they trudged on. His jaw ticked at the sight.

"I know we're young—"

"Yeah," he interrupted. "Really young. Is he even eighteen yet?"

I huffed. "Why do you have to be like that?"

"Like what?" He crossed his arms over his

chest.

"Like everyone else in this town." I shut my locker and clicked the rotary lock in place. "You have no idea what we've been through, how much we love each other. We're still in high school, but I know it's not a mistake."

"I just can't imagine getting married so young," he said.

"Well, it's not your life, Eric. It's mine. If you were a good friend, you'd be happy for me."

"I am happy for you." He touched my arm. "Really. Just surprised is all."

"Well, I was surprised too." I thought back to my initial reaction. "But now Tom and I are on the same page. I get where he's coming from. And it makes perfect sense."

Eric scanned the hallway and then leaned in. "You're not... pregnant are you?"

"Wow." I shook my head. "I wouldn't have expected those words to come out of your mouth."

"It's a reasonable question," he said.

"No, Eric. I hate to disappoint you, but I'm not pregnant."

"I never said you were."

"Look, even if I was, that wouldn't mean we'd be rushing off to get married. Things are different now. The world has changed. Besides, I don't believe in shotgun weddings."

"It was just a question," he muttered. "I'm sorry I asked."

"I don't have a lot of people supporting my decisions right now." I looked him squarely in the eye. "It would be nice if you weren't one of them."

"I'm sorry. I didn't realize my opinion meant that much to you."

I put my hand on his shoulder. "Eric, you're the closet thing I've ever had to a brother. And we were all close growing up. If the roles were reversed, I'd want you to be just as happy as I am. Even if the whole town thought you were crazy."

He narrowed his eyes, clenching his jaw.

"That came out wrong." I looked away.

"Yeah." He took a step back. "This whole town already thinks I'm crazy."

Tom snuck up behind me and planted a kiss on my cheek. His arms came around my shoulders as I laced my fingers through his. "So what do you think?" he asked Eric.

"It seems sudden." Eric flicked his eyes to me. "But I'm happy if you're happy."

"Thank you." I relaxed at the feel of Tom standing behind me.

To my surprise, the boys had become pretty good friends since school started back. Tom had always felt like an outcast. And now that Eric was the new kid in town, they had a lot more in common. For that reason, I'd thought Eric would be quicker to approve.

"How are things goin' with Jeanine?" Tom asked.

"I don't know." Eric put his hands on his hips.

"I think she still hates me."

"She doesn't hate you, Eric," I said. "She just hasn't forgiven you yet."

"Yeah." He broke eye contact. "Well, I better get to class."

"Us too," Tom said. Eric left and Tom took my hand. "You're wearing your ring."

"Yes, I am." I beamed at the sparkle in his eyes.

"What has everyone been saying?" he wondered.

"People talk. But I don't care what they think."

We walked down the hall as he led me to class. "Now we just have to tell your parents."

* * *

I'd thought of the many ways to tell Jeffrey and Eleanor. While I wouldn't call them traditionalists, they would hardly approve of our rush to the altar. Even though—ironically—there was a time when that was the most traditional route to marriage.

My adoptive parents had gotten married later in life. A result of their doctor-lawyer ambitions, no doubt. I'd often wondered if it had thwarted their attempts to have a child of their own. Then again, where would that have left me? If Jeffrey and Eleanor had been able to conceive, I might have never met Tom.

"Did you have a good birthday?" Eleanor asked.

We were seated at the dining room table, and

I'd done everything I could to prolong the inevitable. She asked Tom about my birthday cake, and I was relieved when she took a slice. I'd rather be spending my Friday night alone with him.

But we were engaged now, and my legal guardians needed to know.

"How was the trip?" I said, holding Tom's hand under the table.

"Fine." Eleanor ate a bite of cake. "We saw Eric's parents for a little bit."

"How are they?" So they were out of town, too. Big shocker.

"Good," Jeffrey answered. "They think he's adjusted very well at school."

I looked at Tom and rolled my eyes. Clearly, they didn't have a clue.

"It's nice to have them back in town," Eleanor added. "Such a shame about Emily."

That was a road I had no intention of going down. We needed to talk about something else. "Eric gave me a Georgia bulldogs sweatshirt for my birthday. And Jeanine got me a cashmere sweater."

"That's nice," Eleanor said. "What did you get for her, Tom?"

We exchanged a look, and my heart was pounding. My hands were clammy, my breathing short. I wasn't ready. I didn't want to do this. I wasn't prepared for how they might react. And when it came to Jeffrey, he was so torn up about

Jimmy taking his place that I was already skating on thin ice to begin with.

"Jewelry," Tom said. He glanced my way to see if that was okay.

"Oh." Eleanor finished her cake. "What kind? A necklace?"

"No." Tom shook his head with a smile. "A ring."

There was a lump in my throat, and my stomach was in knots.

"A ring?" That got her attention. "Addie, why aren't you wearing it?"

I averted my eyes, afraid of what she might say.

"She is actually." Tom burned a hole through my face.

"Well, let's see it," Eleanor said.

I looked up and they were both staring at me.

"Is it a promise ring or something?" Jeffrey asked.

I put my left hand on the table. And their eyes dropped like rocks.

"I asked Addie to marry me," Tom said. "And she said yes."

"We're engaged." As the words left my lips, it was like the nail in the coffin.

Jeffrey was speechless, blanching to a starchy pale white. I looked at Eleanor, and she was beside herself. I saw the vein popping out on her forehead, but she hadn't said a word.

"I'm not pregnant," I said. "If that's what you're thinking."

"If you're not pregnant, then why are you engaged?" she asked.

My hand clenched in a fist, and it took all I could not to spontaneously combust.

"We want to get married," Tom said. "We're ready to start our life together."

"At eighteen?" Jeffrey said. "That's awfully young, don't you think?"

"No." I stared at Eleanor.

"Is this about our conversation at dinner the other night?" Eleanor asked. "Are you trying to get back at me just because I didn't jump for joy?"

"No," Tom spoke for me. "I've had this planned. It was a surprise. Addie didn't know."

Eleanor rubbed the back of her neck and stared at the table. Deep down, I wanted her to fight me on this. It wasn't about being defiant. I was an adult now — it was time for her to start accepting my decisions. Whatever they may be.

"I like you Tom," Jeffrey said. "But I think you're just too young. Way too young."

I rolled my eyes as he collected the plates and went into the kitchen. Eleanor sat across the table with a pout on her face. I wasn't afraid of her anymore. My freedom wasn't hers to give.

"What?" I gritted my teeth. "You're not one to be silent."

She shrugged her shoulders and stood up. "I'm not sure what you want me to say."

When she left, I glowered after her. Tom rubbed my back as his eyes settled on my face.

But I darted out of the room and followed her into the kitchen.

"That's all you have to say?" I grabbed her elbow. "I'm getting married. Or did you not hear what we said?"

"I heard what you said, Addie." She turned towards me. "I just think it's a mistake." She started walking away.

"Why?" I asked.

I felt Tom behind me as he came into the kitchen.

Eleanor looked at the two of us. Her eyes raked over Tom and then landed on me. "I don't think you're going to make it in the long run. You don't have what it takes."

It felt like I'd had the wind knocked out of me. "What?"

"You're young now. And you've been through a lot. But you have no idea what it takes to make a marriage work. You may be in love. But you're not soulmates."

She went upstairs as I turned to Jeffrey. But he was just as bad as her, maybe worse. He simply shrugged and then went after her.

There were tears in my eyes. I felt cold, even though I'd been sweating since I walked in the door. To be honest, I can't think of anything worse she could've said to me.

Despite the past eighteen years, tonight took the cake.

"Tom." I looked to him for support. And he

was there. Like he always was.

He pulled me into his arms, and I buried my face in his chest. I couldn't bear the thought of losing him. It was one thing if he were dead. That would be brutal enough.

But if he chose to leave me? Well, that was another thing entirely.

"Let's go home." He burrowed his face in my neck and I nodded.

I packed an overnight bag and left with Tom. They must have heard me walk out the door, but I guess no one cared. Because I sure didn't see them trying to stop me.

An hour later, I sat in the den with a cup of chamomile tea. I'd already showered and put on my pajama bottoms and a sweatshirt. Tom lit a fire and curled up beside me.

"Don't let them get to you," he said. "You can't honestly believe what they said."

I lowered my lashes and studied the flames. I could remember the first time I'd ever stepped foot in this mansion. Even then, it felt like I'd known Tom forever.

"Jimmy doesn't have a problem with it," he said. "Doesn't his opinion count more anyway?"

I took a sip of tea and it burned my tongue.

"Addie." He touched my sleeve. "What do you want to do?"

"I don't know."

He furrowed his brow. "What? But I thought you said—"

"I don't know anymore, Tom." I broke down crying. "I just don't know."

I left my tea in the den and raced upstairs. I was tired. I needed rest.

So I turned down the bed in one of the guest rooms and climbed under the covers. I'd been crying so easily that it felt like I was in physical pain. I looked at the ring on my finger and then slipped my hand under the bedding. Maybe it was all too much, too fast.

"Addie." Tom knocked on the door and came inside. "Baby."

He got in bed and rubbed my arm. I'd been painting an ideal future in my head. I knew what I wanted with him. I wanted it so much that maybe it was too much to have.

He kissed my neck and folded his fingers through mine. "I love you."

I rolled over and looked at him. "I love you, too."

He wrapped me in his arms, tucking my head beneath his chin. We lay like that for a long time, holding each other in the quiet. I closed my eyes and breathed him in.

"We don't have to get married right away, you know." He ran his fingers through my hair. "I don't want you to feel any pressure. I just want you to be happy."

"What if they're right?" I cupped his cheek in my hand.

His golden eyes darted across my face,

blooming with fear and panic.

"What if we don't end up together?" I struggled for breath. "What if we're too young? We don't know what we're doing. And we could end up ruining everything."

"What if we do end up together?" he countered.

"I'm scared." I held his face in my hands.

"Of what?" He pulled me close enough to dissolve the space between us.

"I don't want to lose you," I confessed. "I don't want to ruin what we have."

"You're not going to." He touched my face. "I don't know what the future holds. But I can't imagine a world without you in it. You're mine and I'm yours."

I nodded and wrapped my arms around him.

"Even if it doesn't work out, wouldn't it be worth trying? Don't we deserve a chance? I love you enough to risk that. Because I want you for as long as I can have you."

I traced the shape of his jawline and took a good long look at him.

He was gorgeous. Inside and out. Everything I had ever wanted in a man.

So what was wrong with me? Why was I having second thoughts?

Eleanor had planted the seed of doubt. But what if she was wrong? I'd never known her to be some grand romantic. She knew nothing of true love — the kind Tom and I had.

"Yes," I whispered. "You're the only risk worth taking."

He smiled in the dark, and I leaned in for a kiss. It started soft and sweet, pure innocence. But there was fear raging inside me. The same that had prompted him to propose.

Nothing in life is ever guaranteed. And I just couldn't let the moment pass me by. Not a minute more. I loved Tom — more than life itself. And some things in life you have to grab on to and never let go. Because if you wait, even for a second, they'll be gone for good.

I pushed him onto his back and tangled my fingers through his hair. He didn't fight me, letting his hands roam all over my body instead. I planted kisses down his neck and straddled his lap, working my fingers through the buttons on his shirt.

His hand slid down my thigh as he watched me. I opened his shirt and tucked my hair behind my ears, leaning over to trail a line of kisses down his chest. He rubbed my back and shoulders. Soft, subtle caresses I'd rather feel without any clothing to separate us.

I sat up and pulled my shirt over my head. Something glittered across his amber eyes. Desire? Lust? Passion? I'd take any of them, because it didn't matter. I knew he loved me.

We kissed again, and he traced the contours of my back. I could feel how our bodies were made. Curves and lines. Puzzle pieces meant to fit. We were made for each other.

I was lost in sensation. Every time he kissed me, I shuddered. I wondered if it were the same for him. Deep down, I thought if we went all the way, my body wouldn't be able to handle it.

I hoped I was wrong.

"Addie," he groaned. "Don't stop."

I kissed the stubble on his jaw and it tickled. Then his lips found mine, and he rolled me onto my back. Looking up at the view, I pulled him on top of me with a smile.

"What made you change your mind?" I asked.

He touched his nose to mine and held himself above me. Sensing a flicker of change in his eyes, I grasped his shoulders and dug my nails in. But he leaned back anyway.

"I didn't." He stared at me while I lay there, helpless and disappointed.

"Tom, it's not like someone is going to report us for having sex," I teased.

But he didn't find my joke very funny.

As he pulled away, I sat against the headboard. "I want to share this with you."

He sat on the edge of the mattress, his naked back to me.

I put my hand on his shoulder and then wrapped my arms around him. "Hey."

He touched my hand, and for that I was grateful. But I couldn't take the silence much longer. If we got through this slump, he was going to have to talk to me.

"Maybe it's stupid." He looked back at me. "But I want to marry you first."

It was out of the ordinary, old-fashioned, hardly commonplace nowadays.

"Why is it so important to you?" I asked.

He held my hand in both of his. Then he looked into my eyes and I saw love.

"So much of my life has been out of my control. This is one thing I want to get right." He threaded his fingers in my hair and pressed his forehead to mine.

"All right," I said. "We'll wait until our wedding night. If that's really what you want."

"It is." He stroked the sides of my arms up and down. "And it's going to be worth it."

I kissed him and said, "I thought they didn't make men like you anymore."

"I'm a rare breed," he laughed. He held me in his arms as I nuzzled his chest.

"I guess it will be different if we're already married," I said. "I mean, we've waited this long. Why not wait a little longer?"

"Exactly." He kissed my cheek. "I want it to be special, Addie."

I wrapped my arms around his back and put my head on his shoulder.

"You deserve a white wedding," he said.

It was the nicest thing anyone had ever said to me. And I couldn't believe he thought so much of my purity — like lovemaking of any other kind just wasn't good enough.

I tugged his chin down and whispered, "So do you."

We held each other close and I eventually drifted off in his arms. But not without thinking about everything he'd said. I watched him doze off first and then smiled.

I'd just turned eighteen and I already had a wedding to plan.

Chapter 4

A few weeks later, I came home from school and opened a brand new calendar. It was November, so it made sense to plan for the following year. We couldn't possibly get married now — just seniors in high school. A quickie wedding was out of the picture.

For the first time in a long time, I found myself alone with Eleanor. Jeffrey was still at work, and she'd only come home to get a head-start on packing. Must have been a medical conference or a business trip. By now, I'd learned not to ask. It was all the same to me.

I had to work up the courage to say something to her. She was the only mother I'd ever had, and I didn't know how else to ask. Her advice had to be better than no advice at all.

"Mom." I found her brewing coffee in the kitchen. "Could I talk to you for a minute?"

She looked shocked that I'd said something. I couldn't remember the last time we'd talked. Well, talked the way a mother and daughter are supposed to talk to each other.

When she nodded, I sat down at the table and put the calendar in front of me. She pulled up a chair beside me and took a seat. Her eyes were already looking at the dates.

"I'm marrying Tom, and I know you don't approve. But I was hoping you could help me with the wedding plans. Nothing big now — I just need to decide on a wedding date."

Her cheek twitched as she eyed me carefully. "Why me?"

"Well, you've had your own wedding. And you are my mother."

She released a long-suffering sigh, and I knew she was going to say no. In fact, I'd kind of expected it. But by some miracle, she agreed. I couldn't believe it.

She flipped through the calendar. "You could get married in March. Spring Break is then." She pointed to that week. "That would give you enough time for a honeymoon."

I nodded, but didn't say anything.

"Have you talked to Tom about the possibility of getting married then?" she asked.

"No. He said he doesn't care when we get married. He wants me to set the date."

"Typical groom," she sneered. But her lip turned up with the hint of a smile.

I chuckled, because it was the closest to funny Eleanor ever got.

"Actually, I was hoping to get your advice," I said. "What would you do if you were me? I mean, in my situation. Since we're still in high school?"

She pursed her lips and kept flipping through the calendar. Then she stopped on the month of June, her dark eyes darting from week to week. I folded my hands together, watching and waiting. It was strange to be sitting with her — so calmly like this.

In a weird way, it was what I'd always wanted. For her to spend time with me.

"If I were you, I'd wait until you've graduated to get married. Then you have the whole summer to choose from. And you could take a longer honeymoon if you like."

We looked at dates from the end of May to July. There was solid reasoning behind her suggestions. But I didn't know if Tom wanted to wait that long. And I wouldn't be able to.

At this point, July 31st felt like a year away.

"I was married before," she said. "A long time ago. Before I ever met your father."

My ears perked up. She was never one to spill secrets. I had to listen.

"The marriage only lasted a year. But he was my high school sweetheart."

"What happened?" I asked. "Did he cheat or—"

"No." She looked out the window. "It was nothing like that."

I watched her struggle, giving her time.

"I think that's what made it so painful. No one cheated, no one lied. No one had a substance abuse problem. No one was cruel or abusive."

"Then what was it?" I said.

"Sometimes, it just doesn't work out." She toyed with the watch on her wrist. "We were so young. And we ended up being two completely different people. We didn't really have anything in common. But by the time we figured that out, it was too late."

She took her watch off and flipped it over. There was an inscription on the back.

For my love, Eleanor

She traced the engraving with a smile. Then she put the watch back on and snapped the butterfly latch in place. There were tears in her eyes, but she quietly wiped them away.

"If I've been harsh on you and Tom, it's because I don't want you making the same mistake." She looked out the window again. Leaves were falling off the trees. "I'm happy with your father. But sometimes, I think about how my life used to be. And if we'd tried just a little bit harder, what it could have been."

"But you do love Dad. Don't you?" I wondered.

"Yes, of course I love your father." She looked at me and lifted my chin. "But there is nothing like your first love. It takes a piece of you. And you never get it back."

"I understand." I took a breath. "But I don't think marrying Tom is a mistake."

"Then I'll have to trust that you know best." She looked back at the calendar. "Your father and I will pay for the wedding. I respect your wishes."

I was stunned. "You don't have to do that. Tom and I have our own money. We can—"

"You're the daughter of a doctor, Addison. Trust me, we can afford it."

"I never thought you couldn't," I said. "It's just that I didn't want you to have to worry about it. I mean, you've taken care of me my whole life. You've always paid for everything."

"I know that. But you're my daughter. And your father and I will pay for your wedding."

I gave her a hug that nearly brought me to tears. "Thank you."

"You're young, but you're an adult now. And I'm proud of you."

Her approval meant everything to me. It was what I'd wanted all along.

"Well, I better get ready to go." She stood up. "Let me know when you decide on a date. One of my patients is a wedding planner. And I'm sure she'd cut us a good deal."

"That would be great." I smiled.

"No problem. And Jeffrey will come around. I'm sure he'll be happy to walk you down the aisle." She went upstairs while her words echoed in my head.

Jeffrey wanted to walk me down the aisle. But I'd already asked Jimmy to do it.

* * *

Later that week, I sat in front of the fireplace with Tom. It was after ten o' clock on a school night, but we were just now getting around to talking about the wedding. I pulled out a planner and the new calendar I'd bought for the occasion.

"June would be easier," I said. "By then, we'll be done with school. We wouldn't have to rush the honeymoon. And we'd have plenty of time to get ready for college in the fall."

"Okay." Tom scratched his chin.

"But June seems so far away," I whined. "Doesn't it?"

"As long as I've waited to be with you, yeah."

I narrowed my eyes at him. "When do you want to get married?"

"It doesn't matter what I want. I'm not into all this girly stuff."

"Picking a wedding date is not girly, Tom," I said. "We haven't even started the wedding plans yet, and I already feel like I'm doing this all by myself."

He held his hands up in surrender. "I'm happy with whatever you decide."

"But that's not a decision, Tom. You're just putting it all on my shoulders."

"I'm a guy, okay? I don't care about all this

formal stuff. I would go down to the courthouse and marry you right now if you were okay with it. But I know that's not what you want."

I ran my fingers through my hair. "No, it's not."

"What about March?" he said. "We could get married the weekend before Spring Break and then go on our honeymoon after that."

"Do you really want to get married in the middle of the semester?" I asked.

"I don't care. What do you want to do?"

I wanted to scream. "Why am I the one who has to make all the decisions?"

"Because I want you to be happy!" He watched me stand up.

"Well, you're not making me happy right now." I left the room and sat down at the kitchen table with my head in my hands. A few seconds had gone by when I heard his footsteps. So I rested my head on the table and stared at the wall.

He pulled out the chair beside mine and sighed.

"Do you think we have enough in common?" I asked.

"What? You mean like hobbies?"

I lifted my head and repeated the question.

"Yeah." He nodded. "I think so."

"Eleanor was married before. He was her high school sweetheart. They were only married a year, but I think she's still in love with him. I had no idea."

"Does Jeffrey know?" he asked.

"I guess so. But she never told me until now."

Tom furrowed his brow. "Are you worried—?"

"It just caught me off guard," I said. "I kind of felt sorry for her."

"Just because it didn't work out for them doesn't mean that will happen to us."

"I know that." I put my head back down on the table. I didn't want him to see the tears in my eyes. "I just want to make sure we're doing the right thing."

"Addie, if you're looking for a guarantee, I can't give you one," he said. "But I'll do the best I can to make it work. And if you want it to work as badly as I do..." He rubbed my back as I closed my eyes. "Then it should take care of itself."

"You're right." I took a breath and sat up. "This wedding is just stressing me out."

"Come here." He opened his arms, so I stood up and sailed into them.

As I buried my face in his chest, he cradled my body. "I'm sorry I yelled."

"Me too." He stroked the sleeve of my arm. "I don't want you to be stressed."

"Jeffrey wants to walk me down the aisle. But I already told Jimmy he could."

"Oh. I knew something was bothering you."

"Yeah," I sobbed. "I don't want to hurt him. Even though he hasn't been the best father. I mean, Jeffrey and Eleanor did give me a home. They took me in when no one else would. Doesn't that say something about them?"

"You're just gonna have to find a way to explain it to Jeffrey."

"It's not like they can both walk me down the aisle," I joked.

"That might actually work."

I looked at his face and playfully slapped him on the shoulder.

"Hey!" he laughed. "You're the one who thought of it."

"It's a terrible idea." I looked into his eyes and I knew — the rest didn't matter.

"There is another way." He touched my cheek.

"I'm listening." I smiled, loving the feel of his skin.

"We could go to Vegas and elope."

"No way!" I said. "I'm not getting married by an Elvis impersonator."

"You don't have to," he clarified. "I can just tell them no Elvis."

I giggled and stroked his stubble with the back of my hand.

"What are you thinking about?" he asked.

"You've always been able to make me laugh."

He kissed my forehead. And I touched his cheek.

"I can't wait to marry you," I said. "However it happens."

"Me too." He pulled me in from the back of my neck, brushing his lips over mine. I returned the kiss and begged for another, clinging to him in earnest. We put the brakes on before it got too heated, and he cradled my head on his chest. I was about to close my eyes.

But then the phone rang.

"I'll answer it." Tom wiggled out of the chair.

"No," I whined, grabbing the collar of his shirt.

"Addie," he chuckled. "Come on. It could be important."

I reluctantly agreed and let him go. "Fine."

Tom grabbed the phone on the last ring. It was an old manual phone with a coiled cord connecting it to the wall. I leaned against the chair and watched him answer it.

"Hello?" He waited a beat, while I was left to wonder.

The phone in the kitchen had no caller ID. Answering the phone was a mystery — a surprise caller every time. You never knew who it might be.

"Hello?" He frowned and then hung up, returning to me.

"Who was that?" I asked.

"I don't know," he shrugged. "Must have been a wrong number."

I stretched my arms with a yawn, feeling like a lazy house cat.

"It's late," he said. "Why don't you spend the night?"

I bit my lip and grinned. "I'm not gonna fight you on that."

He took my hand and led me out of the kitchen. I was awfully sleepy, so I crashed into his chest on the way upstairs. Tom pretended to hate it as he picked me up in his arms.

"You're heavy as lead," he muttered. "What have you been eatin'?"

"Hey!" I flicked his arm. To my amusement, he cracked a smile.

"Just teasin' you." He smelled my hair as we reached the second floor.

"That's what I thought."

When he set me down, I felt a tug in my chest. It was like gravity. The urge I felt to move towards him. If we were going to remain celibate, then we had to stop being bedmates.

"Maybe I should sleep in the guest room," I suggested, collecting my things.

Tom furrowed his brow. "What? Why?"

"Do you mind?" I motioned for him to turn around. Then I changed into my pajama bottoms and a long night shirt when he did. "We probably shouldn't even be sleeping under the same roof."

"Addie, we've shared my bed a million times."

I tossed the clothes I'd worn today in my overnight bag. Then I walked around the bed and stood in front of him. "You're the one who wants to wait for marriage, right?"

His eyes widened as it dawned on him. "Right."

"So it's probably not the best idea if we keep sleeping together." I pointed at his bed. "Look how many times we've almost crossed that forbidden line in your bed."

"Forbidden line," he whispered. "You make it sound so provocative."

"You're the one who doesn't want to touch me until I'm your wife."

"Wife?" He grabbed my waist and pulled me in. "Now I like the sound of that."

When he kissed me, I really hated that I had to leave. I always slept better in his arms, but this was the only way we could both get what we wanted. So I gave him a hug and told him goodnight.

Once I left his bedroom, he chased me into the hall. "Where are you going?"

"To sleep in the guest room," I answered. Hadn't we just covered this?

Our kiss hadn't been that good. Not enough to cause rapid memory loss.

"I know. But why are you sleeping in the one downstairs?" he asked.

I leaned against the banister with a sigh. "Because if I..." My cheeks heated with blush. I looked back at him and rolled my eyes. I was almost too embarrassed to say it.

"I just thought if you were close by, it'd be safer," he said.

"If you're right next door to me, I don't know if I can resist." I captured his gaze in the hall. "I don't know if I can keep myself from climbing in your bed and putting my hands all over you."

He gulped and I saw his Adam's apple bob. "Okay."

I moved towards him like a moth to the flame. "But if you think—"

"Nope!" He shook his head. "I think you need to sleep downstairs."

I laughed, because he looked seriously torn. "Are you sure?"

"Yep. In fact, I suggest you head there right now." He pushed me away.

"So much for my safety." I lingered on the steps and looked back at him.

"I'll leave my phone on. Call me if anything happens. And Addie?"

I turned around to catch his last words.

"Lock your door."

I shot him a sexy smirk. "Is that to keep the wolves at bay?"

"No." He kept a straight face. "Just me."

He walked into his bedroom and shut the door. When I heard it lock, desire coursed through me. It was flattering that he felt just as tempted to bed me. I thought about it all the way to the guest room. But then I realized just how big this place was. And that I was alone.

I turned the light on in the hall and peeked inside Daniel's room. It had been so long since I'd allowed myself a glimpse. We'd kept the place just as he'd left it. And if I closed my eyes and took a whiff, it smelled like him.

When I entered the guest room, a shiver shot down my spine. I turned on the bedside lamp and locked the door. Then I approached the windows and closed all the blinds.

I tried not to look through the glass. I tried really hard.

I grabbed a few blankets from the closet and then shut the doors. It was going to be cold tonight. It already was. If the temperature kept dropping, we might get some snow.

After climbing in bed, it took a long time for me to get comfortable. I kept fluffing the pillows and adjusting the covers, hard-pressed to choose a side of the bed. I ended up settling in the middle. But even then, I didn't want to turn out the light.

Eventually, I was too tired to care. So I switched the lamp off and lay down. It had been a long day, and we both had school tomorrow. But I was restless.

Tom felt so far away. And it was hard for me to feel safe when he wasn't near.

An hour later, I was up and puttering around in the kitchen. I couldn't sleep. But I didn't have the heart to go tell Tom. He'd probably fallen asleep as soon as his head hit the pillow. And if he was snoring, why should I disturb him? Then we'd both be miserable.

I made a cup of chamomile tea to help me sleep. Tom had introduced me to the trick when we first met. But it didn't seem to have the same effect when I was sleeping alone.

Calling it a night, I rinsed my cup out and left it in the drain board. Then I returned to the guest room and locked the door behind me. I slipped under the covers and thought about Tom. He'd been my good luck charm. A way to ease away the nightmares.

But I didn't have him tonight. So I'd just have to go it alone.

Just as I felt myself drifting off, the phone rang. I sat up in bed and switched on the light with a groan. At first, the sound didn't register. It was past midnight.

Who would be calling at this hour?

I left the guest room and turned on every light from there to the kitchen. The phone kept ringing, even though I was sure that—by now—it should have gone to voicemail.

Tired and grumpy, I answered the phone with a sad, "Hello."

"Hello, Addison. I've been trying to reach you."

My heart thumped in my chest as I turned around. "Who is this?"

I was watching the doors and windows, afraid for my life.

"Who is this?" I hissed. "Answer me!"

"I believe I knew a companion of yours. Well, I no longer require his services."

I sank down to the floor and put my hand to my chest. "What?" I wheezed.

"News just reached us in Paris. And I'm so sorry to hear of poor Richard's demise."

"Richard?" I said. "I'm sorry, I—I don't know a Richard."

"Ricky," he chimed. "Football player, like his father. American football, that is."

"What do you want?" I cut him off before he could delve deeper.

"Just to relay a message to you Addison, dear."

I took a deep breath and swallowed, ready for the blow.

"I'm just calling to tell you that I found it," he said.

"Found what?" I was panting now, and he must have heard me.

"J'ai trouvé le collier."

"I'm sorry," I hesitated. "I don't speak French."

"I found the necklace."

Chapter 5

I dropped the phone and watched it dangling in the air. Then I took a step back and fell down on the floor. I hadn't recognized the voice, but he knew me. Whoever he was.

"Tom!" I ran upstairs and banged on his bedroom door. "Tom!"

When he opened up, I fell into his arms and cried. I was shaking.

"Hey." He held me close and I breathed a sigh of relief. "What's going on?"

My knees gave way as I collapsed. Tom caught me before I hit the floor. And then he sat me down on his lap, where I nuzzled his bare chest. He was so warm. Now I knew why.

Because I needed him to be. For times like this.

"Did you have a bad dream?" He cupped my cheek in his hand.

"I wish I was dreaming." I looked up with tears in my eyes.

My mind was already peeling back the layers of a summer I thought I'd forgotten.

"After Ricky died, Jeanine found a letter he'd written. It was more like a message."

"Addie." He lifted my chin. "Baby, you're not makin' any sense."

"I would if you'd let me talk." I stood up, but I still felt faint and wobbly.

He grabbed my elbow and sat me down on the edge of the bed.

"The message said, J'ai trouvé le collier. It's French."

"Yeah, I got that part," he said. "What does it mean?"

"I found the necklace."

He blinked twice, as if it took a few heartbeats to register.

"Someone just called the house. He sounded French. And he said the same thing."

He just stared at me, like my words wouldn't process.

"Tom." I squeezed his arm. "I think Ricky had a buyer lined up for the necklace. Someone in Paris. But he said he no longer required Ricky's services."

"Is that because Ricky's dead?" he asked.

"Yes." I wavered by the window. "No."

Tom held on my every word when I turned around.

"Because he already found the necklace."

"Who? This guy you just talked to on the phone?"

"Yeah." I nodded, taking a seat. "But how could that be?"

"I guess it's possible."

"Is it?" I met his golden eyes. "How big is that ocean?"

Thunder broke in the distance as it started to rain. Tom approached the window and looked out, thinking about something. Then he turned back to me and smiled.

"If he already found the necklace, then that's good news." He took my hand and squatted down in front of the bed. "We don't have to worry about someone hounding us."

I squeezed his hand when I felt afraid.

"It's not like before," he said.

"But don't you remember what Jimmy said?" I asked. "How dangerous the necklace is, if it gets into the wrong hands."

"What does that even mean?" He stood up. "Did he ever clarify that for you?"

"No. But he told me to destroy it. And I thought I already had."

"Addie, I wouldn't worry about it." He touched my face. "We can't spend the rest of our lives chasing the past. It's over now. And if someone else has the necklace, good."

"Maybe I should talk to Jimmy about it."

Tom gave me a look.

"It's just to give me some peace of mind," I explained. "So I can really let this go."

"All right," he nodded. "If you think it will help."

"Yeah," I cooed. Then I nuzzled his chest until his arms were around me.

"Have you slept yet?" He rubbed my back.

"Not a wink."

"Aren't you tired? We have school tomorrow."

"I know," I sighed. Tomorrow would be painful. "I'm just ready for the weekend."

"Well, why don't you stay in here?" he suggested. "You're about to fall asleep anyway."

I nodded into his chest and then took a breath. He led me to his bed and turned the covers down. Once I'd climbed beneath them, I put my head on his pillow and sighed.

He hummed a sweet lullaby to help me sleep.

And I was out like a light.

* * *

That Saturday, I got up early and met Jimmy for coffee. I needed someone to talk to about the late night caller. The Frenchman was a stranger. A stranger who knew my name.

"Hey kid." Jimmy already had a table. He stood up and hugged my neck. Then I gave him a quick peck on the cheek and he pulled my chair out for me.

"Thanks for meeting me on such short notice," I said.

"No problem. How was your birthday?" he asked.

I thought about the question. "Full of surprises."

"Nice ring." His eyes lit up with a smile.

"Thank you for the paintings. They're beautiful. You didn't have to do that."

"Sure I did." He took a sip of coffee. "I've got eighteen years of birthdays to make up for."

I blushed and then remembered the reason I'd asked him here.

"Do you remember when you told me about the necklace? About how dangerous it is? Especially if it were to get into the wrong hands."

"Where are you going with this?" he asked. "I thought you already—"

"I did. I threw it in the ocean. But someone found it."

He furrowed his brow.

"Ricky was planning on selling it. He had a buyer lined up in Paris." I showed him the note Jeanine had given me. "That's Ricky's handwriting."

"J'ai trouvé le collier."

I lowered my voice. "It means, 'I found the necklace.'"

"I know what it means." He gave the note back to me.

"I believe Ricky was going to deliver this message to the buyer. But he died before he got the chance." I searched Jimmy's eyes. If he got

81

scared, then I would be terrified.

"What am I missing?" Jimmy wondered.

"Someone called Tom's place in the middle of the night this week. It was a man. And he sounded very French. He knew my name. And he said he wouldn't be requiring Ricky's services anymore. Because he found the necklace himself."

"How is that possible?" he asked. "I mean, I guess it is. But what are the odds?"

"How many miles is it across the Atlantic Ocean? All the way to Paris?"

"Probably a few thousand at least. But I don't know how it could get there that fast."

"It's only been a few months," I said. "Maybe that's not how he got it. What are the chances it would just wash ashore? And that he would even be in the right spot?"

"Sounds like he had someone actively searching for it," he said.

I drummed my fingers on the table. "I wonder if Ricky kept any letters from him."

"I don't know." He looked around the coffee shop. "Maybe."

"I could ask Jeanine. They haven't touched Ricky's room since he died."

"Addie." He reached for my hand. "I don't want you going on a wild goose chase."

"I'm not." I stood up and put my coat on. "But I've got to get to the bottom of this. Tom and I are planning a new life together. I want the past behind us. The best way to do that is to figure out who this guy is. Then I'll know if he's dangerous."

"All right." He got out of his chair and held me at arm's length. "Be careful."

I looked into his eyes and truly meant it. "I will."

* * *

I went straight to Jeanine's without calling first. And while that was probably rude, I didn't think she'd mind. I was just so anxious to uncover the truth that my curiosity had eclipsed everything else.

I rang the doorbell and waited out front. Her parents were just like mine—never at home—so there was no fear of them asking questions. What I didn't expect was to find a blonde hunk answering the door instead. Especially one that I knew so well.

"Eric?" I blinked to be sure. "What are you doing here?"

"I could ask you the same question." He took a step back to let me in.

"I didn't realize the two of you were on speaking terms."

"Well, I've still got some groveling to do. But we're trying to work it out," he said.

"I'm glad." I patted his shoulder and walked around. "Where's Jeanine?"

"Addie!" Jeanine came into the living room. "What are you doing here?"

"Just thought I'd drop by." I stood between them, shifting on my feet.

Now that I was here, I hadn't really thought this through. It might be selfish of me to ask Jeanine to dig up the past. Losing Ricky had been hard on her. Especially since she'd gone through the mourning period twice. Since she'd let Eric into her life again, I thought twice about bringing up Ricky in front of him. Wouldn't that just set them back?

"Actually, I think I left my sweater in your room the last time I was here."

"Oh?" A furrow formed between her brows. "I don't think I've seen it."

"Well, I'll just pop upstairs real quick and check." I headed in that direction. "Don't let me spoil your reunion. Just pretend like I'm not even here."

They were both giving me strange looks. But once I was out of view, I bolted.

I'll admit, I didn't feel great about lying to Jeanine. But for now, it seemed like the right thing to do. I had to find out more about the French buyer. And in a way that wouldn't worry or upset her. Maybe it was divine intervention that Eric happened to be here at the same time.

Once I made it into Ricky's room, I shut the door behind me. He had never been the neatest person. Although that seemed like a foolish thing to focus on now.

He had clothes scattered everywhere. There was a football jersey hanging up in his closet. And the scent of his cologne brought back memories

I'd rather forget.

But I was under the gun here, so I had to act fast.

I tossed my purse on the bed and went for his dresser drawers. Somehow, these clothes were a bit more organized. I wondered if his mother did his laundry when he was alive. (I'd never had the luxury.) But then I saw a box of condoms which ruled that theory out.

I shut the drawers and checked his nightstand. Then the mess under his bed. If there was any paperwork, it had to do with school or football. I'd almost given up before I turned to his closet. He had cleats on the floor and athletic gear hanging up.

If Ricky had been keeping correspondence, then where would he put it?

Kneeling down, I moved things around in his closet until I could actually see the floor. It was a pretty beige carpet — the kind that would stain at the mere sight of blood.

As I ran my hand over the carpet, it lifted at the corner. I leaned over and pulled from that end. And a square piece of carpet came up. It was about the size of a football.

There was a hole in the floor. And when I looked down, I saw a Bible inside.

I heard footsteps on the stairs and panicked. "Addie?"

So I grabbed the Bible and shoved it in my purse. Then I put the carpet down and left the room as it was. When I walked into the hall, Eric and Jeanine spotted me.

"Couldn't find my sweater," I said. "Must have left it at Tom's."

I hoped they couldn't hear that I was out of breath.

"We were about to watch a movie," Jeanine said. "You're welcome to stay."

"No, I better get going." I headed for the stairs. "I didn't mean to barge in on you."

"No, you're fine." Jeanine smiled. "It feels like we haven't hung out in a while."

"Yeah. I've just been busy. The wedding plans and all." I avoided eye contact. "But I'll see you at school." I gave them each a hug. "I didn't mean to ruin your date."

They walked me out the front door and I left in a hurry. Cool as a cucumber just wasn't my style. Especially when I'd just stolen something as sacred as a dead man's Bible.

I thought about pulling over on the side of the road. Or sneaking a peek at a red light. I was so anxious that I couldn't stand it. Surely, there was more than scripture in the book.

But I waited until I was in safe quarters to investigate. For some reason, I wanted to unravel the mystery alone. Then I would have time to process it all before I went to Tom.

The minute I walked in the front door, Jeffrey was waiting for me.

"Hey." He'd been sitting in the recliner and

pretending to read a book.

"Hey." I passed him and headed for the stairs.

"Do you have a minute?" he asked. "I was hoping we could talk."

Stopping in my tracks, I turned around and dropped my purse on the couch. "Sure. What do you want to talk about?"

"It's about your wedding. Your mother spoke to me today. And I think I was too harsh on you. You've always been a good kid. And Tom has, too. I shouldn't be so against you getting married. Before I know it, you'll be out of here. So I wanted to give you my blessing."

It was unexpected, but I was flattered. "Thank you."

"We'll also be taking care of everything for the wedding," he said.

"Oh." Eleanor had said the same thing. "Thank you. I really appreciate it."

"It's the least we can do. After all, you are our daughter."

I forced a smile, mainly because I could tell where this was headed.

"Well, I'll let you go," he said. "I know you're busy."

Now I felt guilty. So I kissed him on the cheek and then resumed my plans.

"Oh and Addie?" he called. "Your mother talked to me."

I turned back on the stairs.

"And I would love to walk you down the aisle

at the wedding."

I was going to be sick. "Oh."

"It's my duty to see my little girl off on her big day."

I nodded but didn't say anything. I didn't have the heart to break it to him just yet. So I went to my room and shut the door behind me. I'd have to deal with that later.

My heart was pounding as I sat down on my bed. I turned my purse over and poured all the contents out. When the Bible hit the mattress, I grabbed it and held my breath.

I opened it. Someone had cut out the middle in the shape of a coffin. It would have been the perfect place to hide anything valuable. Money. Notes. The necklace.

But there was nothing. No jewelry, no message. Not the first dollar or coin.

It was empty. And I had a funny feeling that it hadn't always been like that.

Whatever used to live in that paper coffin was quite simply... gone.

Chapter 6

I kept the Bible for three days before I told anyone. I don't know why I felt so weird about it. Ricky was gone. And I'd only taken it for investigative purposes.

Apart from the hole in the middle, the book was in mint condition. As ironic as it sounds, the leather smelled like heaven. It was dark green and awfully smooth for being pigeon-holed in a teenage boy's closet. There was an inscription on the back in gold.

I flipped through the tissue pages — so fragile a gentle breeze would leave a tear. And I thought about the last time I'd been to church. It had been mostly funerals lately. But I wouldn't mind attending a regular service. Or a wedding, perhaps. Not my own, of course.

I'd failed to anticipate Jeffrey and Eleanor coming around so quickly. I was flattered by their offer to pay for the wedding. But there was the issue of being walked down the aisle.

Which father held the right?

Jeffrey had given me a legal name, food and shelter. Private tuition. Credit cards.

And then there was Jimmy. He'd come later in my life. But he was the real deal.

In my heart, I knew I wouldn't be satisfied if Jeffrey did it. He'd provided the most basic needs, but there was a lot of gray area—many times he'd missed out.

Jimmy should have made contact sooner. But maybe he felt like he couldn't. He'd been kept in the dark until it was too late. And I'd already been given away.

I twisted the ring on my finger and paced the floor. My whole life, I'd thought weddings were about two people: the bride and groom. But I was wrong. You had to get entire families involved. And that was the problem. Too many people with loud opinions who wouldn't take no for an answer.

Part of me felt bad for thinking that way. Because Tom didn't even have a family.

So maybe I shouldn't have been complaining about mine.

Regardless, I would have to talk to Jeffrey at some point. I couldn't just let him jump in and take a place that had already been claimed. Deep down, I believe Jimmy would have raised me himself, if he'd known that I existed. If Josette had told him.

I'd always heard she ran away. I assumed she was living on the street until someone found her nine months pregnant and homeless. I couldn't believe that was me—the baby inside her. Even now, it made me feel helpless and afraid. Like I was lost.

To be honest, I wasn't feeling great. Since my eighteenth birthday, everything had been so up and down. One minute, I was soaring high on a love cloud with Tom. The next, it all came crashing down. I was still living in the past—afraid of what might be lurking in the shadows of the forest.

Would it always be like this?

Would I always be so afraid of life?

When Tom came over that afternoon, I was lying in bed. I felt cold and restless. Ever since the phone call from Paris, I'd been having anxiety, nightmares, negative thoughts. Stealing Ricky's Bible hadn't helped.

But I couldn't shake the sound of the Frenchman's voice.

J'ai trouvé le collier.

I found the necklace.

It felt like a noose around my neck. Would I ever escape it?

Would there ever come a time when someone wasn't asking about the necklace?

"It just looks like a Bible to me," Tom said. "French translation."

"Yes, but did you look inside?" I asked.

"Someone cut out the middle."

"Yeah." Tom looked at the hole in the pages. "He Shawshanked this one."

"Did you just turn The Shawshank Redemption into a verb?" I said.

Tom thought about it.

"Never mind. What do you think Ricky was doing with a Bible like this?"

Tom shrugged, taking a seat beside me. "The man from Paris probably gave it to him. Maybe Ricky used it to store money." He flipped through the pages. "I'll bet he was going to use this to hide the necklace and then smuggle it into Paris."

"But how did this guy even hear about it? You think Ricky was trying to sell it on the black market or something? I mean, where do you find buyers for stolen gems?"

"I don't know." Tom set the Bible down. "But I don't really see how it matters now."

"Yeah. You're probably right." I leaned back and the Bible toppled to the floor.

"I'll get it," Tom said with a smile.

"Sorry." I watched him bend over and blushed. All too soon, he would be mine.

He stood up with the open book in his hands. Then he flipped a few pages. There was a curious look on his face, as his amber eyes scanned letter by letter.

"What's going on?" I knelt down on the mattress.

He caught my gaze and then handed me the

Bible. "Look at that."

I looked at Tom, because I was too afraid to see what he'd found.

There was something in his eyes I'd never seen before. For the first time, he wasn't afraid of something new he'd discovered. Was it possible that secrets no longer posed a threat? If they proved to be any more dangerous, we wouldn't make it out alive.

There was a page at the beginning of the Bible. A line for the owner. And a name.

My eyes widened at the surname. I'd heard it before. More than once.

"Beaumont?" I stared at Tom. "Does that mean...?"

"Addie, I don't think this guy is an enemy, or even a friend." He sat down and took my hand. "I think he's related to you."

My mind was an explosion of thought. Beaumont was the name Josette had used. It was the same one on my birth certificate. Was this Antoinette's family?

"He must be a distant relative of yours," Tom suggested.

"But what would he have to do with the necklace?" I asked.

"I don't know." Tom scratched his brow. "I don't know."

I looked at the name again.

Edmond Pierre Beaumont

"Who is this guy?" I shut the book. I felt

excited, overwhelmed.

"I don't know. But I'd figure it out if I were you." Tom went downstairs to start dinner.

So I pulled out my laptop and typed the name into Google. An image popped up of a wealthy aristocrat. He was eighty six years old, currently living in Paris, France.

I read his biography until my eyes grew tired. He was born to a family of aristocrats. A third generation blue blood. He lived in a castle on a 3,000 acre estate just south of Paris.

My heart was pounding as I clicked through his photos. He'd been an avid hunter and horseman, but old age had slowed Beaumont down. I stopped when I saw him close up.

The picture must have been taken ages ago. He was outside on the front lawn standing by a black horse. I zoomed in on the photo. Again and again and again. And then I saw it.

Green eyes. Just as unusual as mine. Glistening like emeralds, deep as the jungle.

I shut my laptop and thought about Antoinette's portrait. She'd possessed the same green spheres of light. Beautiful enough to capture Daniel's eye. And Jimmy's as well.

Daniel once said my eyes were as rare as the necklace itself. I'd never quite understood what he meant by it. At the time, I hadn't known he was my grandfather. So I just thought he was being nice—paying a compliment to the girlfriend of his only grandson.

I shook my head and ran my fingers through my hair. It was too much all at once.

There was no way. I couldn't have this whole other family. A real family.

Just like I'd always wanted. Not now.

It didn't make any sense. Welcoming Jimmy into my life had been enough. I didn't even know these people. These distant Parisian relatives. Did they even love me?

And what did they want? Just a direct line to the necklace? The one I'd tossed in the ocean Titanic style? I'd only been hoping to obliterate the darkness from my life forever.

But what if I'd opened a portal? And welcomed it back in? Without even knowing it?

The doorbell rang so I scurried downstairs to grab it. Jimmy had dropped by without calling first, which I didn't mind at all. Jeffrey and Eleanor were out, which was probably for the best. They had yet to warm to the idea of me having a biological father.

While Tom finished dinner, I invited Jimmy into the living room. We sat down, and I racked my brain for the best way to break the news to him. Surely, he must know something.

"Sorry to just show up like this. But I'll be out of town at a conference for a few days. I wanted to see you before I left." He sat down in Jeffrey's recliner, but I didn't stop him.

"It's fine, really." I forced a smile. "I'm glad you're here. I wanted to talk."

He rested his hands on the arms of the recliner. "Sure thing, kid. Shoot."

"Did you ever meet Josette's family? I mean, besides Daniel?" I asked.

"No." He shook his head. "Her mother died when she was young. And I believe she had a brother, too. I think he died when he was a baby. It was just Daniel, really."

I rubbed my jaw and then moved to the end of the couch.

"But her mother, Antoinette, she was from France," he said.

"What? I thought she was American. Daniel said they met at school."

"That's right. Her family was from France. They were only supposed to be here for a few years. Something related to the father's work. But when it was time for the family to go back home to France, Antoinette refused. I think she ran away from home."

"Why?"

"Because of Daniel," he said. "She wanted to be with him. So they got married. And she stayed here. I don't think the family ever forgave her for it."

I stood up and walked around the room. I couldn't sit still anymore.

"Josette was born here. I don't know if she ever even met her French relatives."

"The guy that called the other night from Paris? I think he's one of them," I said.

"One of your distant relatives?" When I nodded, he asked, "How can you be so sure?"

I showed him the Bible. "Beaumont. It was Antoinette's maiden name."

"Where did you find this?" He opened the Bible, flipping through the holey pages.

"It was in Ricky's closet. I think the buyer he'd contacted is my family."

"I don't know, Addie. After Antoinette left, I think they kind of disowned her."

"So what does that mean?" I looked him in the eye. "I might have a family out there. People who are related to me that I've never even met. Isn't that—I don't know..."

"Addie, these people are strangers to you," he said. "And the only reason the man called is because of the necklace? Why didn't he tell you who he was on the phone?"

"I don't know. Maybe he thought I already knew," I said.

"So what? Now you want to go and meet them?" He stood up.

"What is wrong with that? If they're my family, shouldn't I be able to?" I snapped.

He sighed and looked out the window.

"Why did Josette leave you?" I asked. "Why did she disappear?"

"I don't know," he hissed. "But I don't see why you want to go digging up the past."

"Because they can tell me about my grandmother! They can tell me about the life I never even knew I had. Can't you understand that I need something permanent? I need a history! Roots that explain where I came from. You of all people should understand that."

Tom walked into the room. "Dinner is ready."

I took a breath. "Can you give us a minute?"

"Yeah." I heard his footsteps as he went into the kitchen.

"Look, I don't expect anything from them, all right? But what if they are my family? What if they do want to meet me? What if he was looking for the necklace so he could keep it in the family where it belongs? Haven't you ever thought of that?"

Jimmy flared his nostrils. "I think you'd be safer on US soil."

"I'm not going over there, Jimmy! God, you act like I'm moving in with them."

He grabbed my arms. "I just want you to be safe. I haven't done a very good job of watching out for you, and I'm sorry. But I'm not gonna stop protecting you now."

"You don't need to protect me." I took a step back. "I'm perfectly fine."

"You know, just because you're eighteen now with a fiancé doesn't mean you have it all figured out. You have a lot of life ahead of you, and you have a lot to learn."

I gasped at his snide remark. "What are you saying? That I'm stupid?"

"No! Of course not. I just think you need to be

a little more careful."

"Err on the side of caution?" I said. "And where has that gotten me so far?"

"Look, I have nothing against your mother's family."

"No, it's my grandmother's family that you seem to have a problem with!"

"You don't know what you're getting into." He was crowding me. "I told you to stay far away from that necklace and everyone affiliated with it. Don't walk right back into a trap!"

"What trap?" I yelled. "No one is trapping me! He already has the necklace!"

"Then why even talk to him then?" He paused so I could take a breath.

"Jimmy, I'm eighteen. I'm an adult now. And up until a few months ago, I didn't even know who you were. If it weren't for Daniel, I would have never gone to the institute. He's the only reason I got accepted into that program. And that's the only reason I met you."

"What are you saying?" he asked.

"I'm saying you didn't try awfully hard to make me a part of your life. So why are you criticizing my family for doing the exact same thing?"

He narrowed his eyes.

"You can't tell me what to do anymore. You don't have the right."

He looked down and nodded. Then he grabbed his coat and headed for the door. Jeffrey walked in at the same moment. And it took all I could to keep quiet.

"Oh, hi!" Jeffrey extended his hand. "Nice to finally meet you."

They'd seen each other before, but never been formally introduced.

Jimmy shook his hand. And then he turned to look back at me.

"By the way, thank you so much for letting me walk Addie down the aisle," Jeffrey chimed. "I thought sure she'd ask you first, but I'm honored to have the privilege."

Jimmy's dark eyes pierced through me, as I saw Tom enter the foyer.

"I promise I'll take care of our girl," Jeffrey said.

"Yeah." Jimmy patted him on the back. "You do that."

Tears stung the back of my eyes. Harsh, prickly jabs. Even in my chest, it burned.

Jimmy left and closed the door behind him. When Jeffrey greeted Tom, I marched into the foyer with vengeance. Tears were streaming down my cheeks at this point.

"For the record, I didn't ask you first," I said. "I asked Jimmy."

I felt bad for breaking his heart like that. But I had to come clean at some point. And it might as well be now.

I ran upstairs and slammed my bedroom door behind me. Then I sank down on the floor and cried. For so long, I'd been dying for a family. A

parent. A father.
    Now I had two. And they both hated me.

Chapter 7

By December, I was too focused on finals to think of anything else. But my mind wandered occasionally. I took study breaks and Googled the Beaumonts in France.

I must have had Edmond's biography memorized by now. But it was just so fascinating. His family history. I suppose it was my family history as well. Or at least, I hoped it was.

I kept these fascinations a secret. Even from Tom.

It just felt like no one would want to hear it.

I hadn't spoken to Jimmy. Or Jeffrey. And Eleanor had been away.

But I didn't want to dump my obsession on Tom's shoulders. He'd been the one to suggest it— that Beaumont might not be a stranger. That he might be a relative.

I wanted to believe it so much. Every time I

saw his photo, it just felt real.

I thought my hope of meeting distant relatives was lost forever. A pipe dream. A fantasy. Maybe I wanted a big family so badly that I'd conjured one up in my head.

But then Tom received a letter in the mail. From France. It was addressed to me.

I tore through the envelope, my heart beating a mile a minute. There was a seal on the back made from hot red wax. I ran my finger over the breathtaking B. It was beautiful and bold, an elegant font. I wondered if they had a family crest. Was this it?

"Well." I felt Tom's eyes on me. "What does it say?" he asked.

"It's from Edmond." I read the letter so fast that I had to go back a second time. "He's invited us to stay with him for Christmas. He has a castle near Paris."

"Us?" Tom looked over my shoulder. "You mean I'm invited too?"

"Your name's on the letter." I showed it to him. "See."

"Hmm." Tom didn't say anything for a minute.

"What?" I was quick to judge, because I'd thought he'd be as thrilled as I was.

"It's just... how does he know anything about us?" he asked.

"Ricky." I looked into Tom's eyes, but he would need more convincing.

"And you really believe he's related to you.

This Beaumont guy?"

"Yes." I nodded. "I really do. Why don't I call him and ask?"

"He gave you his number?"

"Yeah, it's right here in the letter." I pointed at the ten digit number.

Tom shook his head and took a step back. "This is crazy."

"No, it's not. It's exciting! Can't you see how happy this makes me?" I asked.

He searched my face and took a breath. "Yeah. But I wouldn't dare let you go alone."

"He's not asking me to. You're invited, remember? Shouldn't that make you feel better?" I squeezed his hand, but he didn't squeeze mine back.

"I don't know. I'm with Jimmy on this one. All this time, where have they been?"

"Couldn't you say the same thing about him?" I snapped.

Jimmy was still a sensitive subject, even now. I hated that we'd become estranged almost as quickly as we'd met. But he had to let me explore the branches on my family tree. I'd been deprived of blood relations for so long, that I didn't even know what it felt like.

"So... does this mean we're going to France for Christmas?" Tom asked.

"Well, not if you don't want to. But Jeffrey and Eleanor have never been big holiday people. They're always busy with work. What if this is my first real Christmas?"

He nodded.

"What?" I probed. "You still don't want to go."

"It's not that." He held my hands. "I just want to make sure you're being careful. I mean, how many times have we been lied to? Is there a way to check up on all this before we make plans to fly out there?"

"I've already researched the heck out of him. But I don't have any proof that we're actually related. It's all just assumptions, really. I'd like to trust my gut on this one. I don't think I'm wrong."

Tom stroked my cheek. Then he pulled me into his arms and sighed.

"I know it doesn't make any sense," I whispered. "But I really think these people could be my long lost relatives."

"I know." He tucked a lock of hair behind my ear. "I just don't want you getting hurt."

"Well, why don't I just call him and see how that goes?" I suggested.

Tom looked at his watch. "It's ten p.m. in Paris. They're six hours ahead of us."

"Do you think it's too late to call?" I wondered. "I could try him tomorrow."

So that's what I did.

It was Saturday, so I placed the call as soon as I got up. My heart was pounding, and I felt sure he'd hear the shakiness in my voice. But there was no going back now.

After the first ring, there was a lot of fast French. So I asked if anyone spoke English.

"Beaumont residence," a melodious voice clipped. "May I ask who is calling?"

"Addie, I mean, Addison." I held my breath. "Smith. Addison Smith."

"You wish to speak to—"

"Edmond Pierre," I swallowed and felt like crying. "Monsieur Beaumont."

"You wish to speak to the count?" she said.

"Yes," I sighed. "The count."

I'd forgotten he had one of those fancy titles. Was that how I was expected to address him? The Count of... Well, I had no idea. Maybe the name of his estate. The only knowledge I had of counts was from World History and The Count of Monte Cristo.

"Just a moment, Addison. He's been expecting your call."

My heart pounded like a drum. He'd been expecting my call. He wanted to hear from me. He wanted to meet me. I could have leapt off the roof, I was so excited.

It was finally happening.

"Addison," he said. "Good afternoon."

"Well, it's still morning in Savannah."

He chuckled, and I rather liked the sound of his laugh.

"I'm afraid we didn't get off on the right foot, the last time I called."

"No," I agreed. "I'm afraid not."

"Do you know who I am?" he asked.

I could hear my heart in my chest. "I believe so."

"I'm your uncle. Your grandmother was my baby sister."

"Antoinette?" I clarified.

"Yes. Antoinette," he said.

So that made him my great uncle. It was wonderful news.

"Why didn't you tell me who you were?" I wondered. "When you called?"

"I was under the impression that you and Richard were intimate?"

I rolled my eyes. What had Ricky told him?

"He was never a friend. But I could see how he'd leave you with that impression."

"Yes, well, I never heard all the details. But I'm sorry for his loss."

"How did you come in contact with him?" I asked.

"Well, I've actually been trying to find you for a few years now."

"Oh?" I was surprised.

"Yes, I'd heard that Antoinette had a granddaughter."

"So why now?" I wondered. "After all this time?"

"When Antoinette married your grandfather, our father cut her out of the family."

"Why?" They were in love. What was so wrong with her marrying Daniel?

"He wanted her to stay with us in France. We are royalty after all."

"But she wanted to be with Daniel," I said.

"Our father made her choose between royalty and love. And then when she chose love, he punished her for it. I think because he felt like she'd chosen him over the family."

"Why didn't I ever know anything about this? Why didn't anyone tell me?" I asked.

"Because there was no one to tell you. I hired a private detective to find you."

"You did?" I couldn't believe it.

"Yes, when Antoinette married, the name Beaumont disappeared. And then your grandfather, Sutton. Well, you didn't have that name either. Adoption tends to complicate matters."

"Yes." I liked his accent. It was rich and royal. "I have a question."

"I'm sure you have many, Addie."

"Well. When you called, it was only to tell me about the necklace."

He didn't say anything.

"I guess what I'm asking is... Have you been looking for the necklace or for me?"

"I know about the necklace. And I'd heard it had gone missing years ago. But don't be mistaken, dear. You didn't lead me to the necklace. The necklace led me to you."

"How is that?" I asked.

"The detective I hired. He went to Savannah to

find you. While he was there, he came across Richard, your friend. He was trying to sell the necklace so he could flee the country with you."

Blush flamed my cheeks.

"The minute I heard about the necklace, I knew it must lead back to you. Antoinette was the last person who had been seen wearing it. So I had my man follow Richard. And then he followed you."

"But that necklace should be at the bottom of the ocean," I said.

"He saw you throw it in. And when you went inside, he dove in after it."

I rubbed my forehead with the palm of my hand. I'd been so clueless about everything.

"So you have the necklace now?" I asked.

"Yes. We'll be donating the necklace to the Louvre. Have you heard of it?"

"Yeah." I smiled. It was only the largest art museum in the world.

"Well, that's why I've invited you to Paris. We'd like you at the ceremony."

"What?" It all sounded too good to be true. I hoped I wasn't dreaming.

"Yes, to commemorate the piece. I believe donating it to Louvre is what my sister would have wanted. And they have plenty of security to keep it protected."

"Why didn't you tell me any of this the first time we spoke?" I asked.

"Richard led me to believe you already knew

who I was."

"For the record, I wouldn't believe anything he told you."

"All right then," he chuckled. "Do you have any other questions?"

"Is there any other reason you want me in Paris?" I asked. "Apart from the ceremony?"

Did he truly want to reconnect with his long lost niece?

Or was it all about the necklace?

"The necklace is a bonus, my dear. You are the grand prize. Why do you think I invited you to the castle for Christmas? You're our family. We want to meet you."

Tears burned the back of my eyes. "I want to meet all of you, too."

"Excellent, then it's all settled. I'll book you two plane tickets to Paris."

"Uncle Edmond, I don't expect you to pay for our tickets."

"Of course I am!" he insisted. "I understand that you have a man in your life?"

"Yes," I grinned. "Tom. We're engaged."

"Well, that's wonderful! It's Christmas and there is no reason why I can't pay for my great niece and her fiancé to come to the castle for a visit. It's all being arranged."

"I don't know what to say. It's all happening so fast."

"When does your Christmas break begin?" he asked.

"Third week of December. I'll look up the exact date."

"Why don't you call my assistant, Cosette?" He gave me her number. "She'll arrange all the details."

"I will. Thank you so much. I'm really looking forward to Christmas!"

"We are too. And don't forget that fiancé of yours. We'd all love to meet him!"

"Well, I guess I'll be seeing you soon then," I said. "Goodbye."

"Goodbye Addison."

I hung up and jumped for joy. Then I ran through the woods to tell Tom all the details. He'd been skeptical at first, but now even Tom was convinced. The connection was real.

I had a family.

* * *

A week later, I caught Jeffrey and Eleanor at a rare time. They were both home.

Tom was by my side, because we'd decided to finally tell them. That I had family in France. That they wanted me there with them for Christmas. That they'd invited Tom to come, too. And that, no matter what Jeffrey and Eleanor thought, I was going anyway.

I'd never had a rocky relationship with Jeffrey. But he was still mad.

Why did he want to walk me down the aisle so badly? He'd never been eager to fulfill the duties of a good father. Especially my father. So why now?

I told Eleanor everything, and she seemed impressed. About Louvre. The ceremony. Everything Uncle Edmond had said. It was a dream of mine to be reunited with them.

"Well, if he's going to pay for your plane ticket, then I don't see a problem," she said.

I looked at Jeffrey. But he had yet to raise his head. Maybe he was still sulking.

"So you really don't mind?" I asked. "If I'm not here for Christmas?"

Don't get me wrong, I was happy she'd said yes. But I'd thought at least one of them would be a little disappointed that I would be overseas for the holidays. Was I finally seeing the truth? That they'd never cared about me in a close, familial way in the first place?

"No." Eleanor frowned. "You're eighteen now. You can do whatever you want."

I looked at Tom and he smiled. We were finally getting what we wanted.

"But we've decided that we no longer want to pay for the wedding," she said.

"What?" I barked. "All because I want to spend time with my uncle in Paris?"

"No, we discussed this earlier. If you want to learn more, speak to your father." She left me standing there, while I turned to Tom. Jeffrey was sitting by the window, quiet as a mouse.

"Dad." I looked at him. "What's going on? Is this all because of Paris?"

"No." He drummed his fingers on the table. "It's about Jimmy."

"What are you talking about?" I asked.

"I'm not paying for your wedding if that man is going to walk you down the aisle."

"That man? Oh, you mean my father!" I'd never been so quick to anger.

"He's never done anything for you. I'm the one who's been here. I'm the one who's provided for you. Food and clothing. A roof over your head. If it'd been up to him, I guess you would've starved to death."

"He didn't even know I existed until after you'd adopted me!"

"And there you go again, taking up for him." Jeffrey left the room.

"I never meant to hurt you." I went after him. "But what Eleanor told you was a lie. I did ask Jimmy first. And I didn't have the heart to tell you yet."

Jeffrey turned back at the staircase. "My decision is final. The only way I'm paying for your wedding is if I'm the one walking you down the aisle."

"But that's not fair! You're making me choose between the two of you," I cried.

"How can I, Addie?" he asked. "You've already made your decision."

"Fine! Don't pay for my wedding! I'll pay for it myself!" I ran up to my room and slammed the door. Then I started packing for Paris. As soon as finals were over, I'd be on a plane out of the country. I couldn't wait to get thousands of miles away from here.

Chapter 8

For the first time, finals felt like a breeze. I aced every one with flying colors. It wasn't that I usually performed poorly. But I'd never had something to look forward to at the end of the semester. Not like this.

Tom did just as well. And we were delighted to begin our new life together. I'd been staying at the mansion so we could stay up late studying. When we returned from Paris, I was thinking of moving in permanently. What would Tom think? I hadn't asked him yet.

Maybe because I was afraid he would say no.

Jeffrey and Eleanor were refusing to pay for the wedding. But I wouldn't let that stop me. I could break into my trust early and use that money to pay for the wedding. I'd already scheduled an appointment with Daniel's attorney.

Deep down, I knew that wasn't the way Daniel

had wanted it. He'd intended for that money to take care of college, a house, living expenses, children. But I was eighteen now.

And I had to make these decisions for myself. I could only hope that Daniel would approve. Since Tom was still a minor, it was up to me to convince the trustee to release a portion of the money now. It was for our wedding. How could he refuse?

Tom had been left with just as much inheritance. It was only because of my age that we would have to start dipping into mine. I wondered how much a wedding would cost.

Surely, nothing elaborate would suit us. I wanted a small wedding with only a handful of people there. Now that I thought about it, I wasn't at all opposed to the courthouse.

But maybe it was too soon to think of a wedding now. We had Paris to worry about.

It was our last day in the states. And we decided to spend it with Eric and Jeanine. They were extremely supportive about Paris. Which made me wish they could go, too.

Because of her father, Jeanine said it wasn't the money. Her parents wouldn't let her live if she ditched them on Christmas Day. Eric echoed much of the same.

Part of me envied them for that. I didn't know what the feeling was like—to have parents who really wanted you there on national holidays. And who celebrated your wedding.

Once Eric and Jeanine bid us adieu, we were on our way. Our bags were already in the car, so we could have gone straight to the airport. But I had one last stop to make.

I'd never mended fences with Jimmy. And I hated leaving the country while we were on the outs. It left a bad taste in my mouth. Especially since Paris was where I'd be reconnecting with loved ones. Actual flesh and blood. Biological kin who really loved me.

I stood on Jimmy's doorstep and knocked. It was freezing out here in the dark. The weatherman said it might snow, but I'd have to see that to believe it.

When he opened up, I gave him a small smile. "Hi."

He pulled me into a hug and patted my back. I knew all had been forgiven.

"I'm sorry to just drop in on you like this," I said.

Tom walked up as Jimmy led us inside. We sat down in the living room. And Jimmy brought us milk and cookies. Like the Santa Clause I'd never had growing up.

"So what's up?" Jimmy dunked a chocolate chip cookie in a glass of milk.

"Well. We've decided to go to Paris."

Jimmy coughed on his cookie and then swallowed, taking a slow drink.

"Who are you staying with?" he asked.

"I did a lot of research, and I've talked to him

on the phone several times."

"Who?" Jimmy asked.

"I have an uncle in Paris. A great uncle actually. He was my grandmother's brother. And he's a count."

"Well." Jimmy brushed cookie crumbs off his hands. "I don't know how to compete with that."

"It shouldn't be a competition," I said. "You're family, just like him."

"And what about the necklace?" he pressed.

"They are donating it to Louvre. And they invited me to go to the ceremony."

Jimmy nodded. "I'm glad they're giving it away. You won't be in danger anymore."

I smiled. "I just wanted you to know that they are my family. I'm sure of it."

He shrugged. "You're probably right. I feel better knowing that about the necklace."

He had a point. Most of the danger in my life had been caused by the necklace. If it were locked away in a museum, who could threaten me over it? It was out of my control.

"So..." Jimmy smirked. "When will you lovebirds return?"

"New Year's," Tom answered. "We have school the next day."

"Christmas won't be the same without you," Jimmy said.

"You've never had a Christmas with me," I smiled.

"I know. But it would have been nice." He

frowned. "I don't want you to stay here on account of me, Addie. Go to Paris. And you can tell me all about it when you get back."

"Really? I wish you could come with us." I would miss him.

"I know. But we can spend Christmas together next year," he said.

"You've got a deal." I stuck out my hand and we shook on it.

"So Tom," Jimmy said, "when's the big day?"

"We haven't picked a date yet," Tom replied.

"Actually, we kind of lost our financing, so to speak," I said.

"What?" Jimmy furrowed his brow.

"Jeffrey won't pay for the wedding unless he can walk me down the aisle."

Jimmy sat back in his chair, looking off. "I wouldn't mind if—"

"It's my wedding," I demanded. "And I want you to do it."

"I'm flattered, kid. Really I am. But I don't know if I can give you the kind of wedding you're looking for. I'm happy to help, but I'm no doctor or lawyer."

"I don't expect you to pay for anything, Jimmy," I said.

"But what if I want to?" he asked.

"I have some inheritance money Daniel left me. Now that I'm eighteen, I could use—"

"Addie, stop," Jimmy said. "When you get back from Paris, let's talk about the kind of wedding you want to have. You've got to let me contribute. At least something."

"Well," Tom spoke up. "We were thinking of having a small wedding."

"Look, kid, as long as this isn't some hundred grand blow-out, I've got you covered."

I blinked at Jimmy. "Really?"

"Really."

I leapt into his arms and gave him a hug. "Thank you."

There were tears in my eyes. It meant so much to have him take part in this. And it wasn't about the money. I'd wanted an active father for so long. Now I finally had one.

"Don't get all choked up now," Jimmy said. "You two have a flight to catch."

I leaned back and dried my eyes.

"When you get home, we'll figure out all the details," he promised.

"Thanks Jimmy." I looked back. "I meant to call you Dad."

"I know everything's been real screwed up."

"Dad, you don't have to—"

"But you kids have got somethin' special." He put my hand in Tom's. "Don't ever let anyone take it away from you. Especially at your age, this kind of thing just doesn't happen."

"Then how did it, do you think?" I asked.

"I don't know." Jimmy shook his head. "But if I were you, I'd never let go."

"I won't," Tom said.

I turned my head. He was staring at me with love in his eyes. Like I was the most beautiful thing he'd ever seen. He didn't just love me. He cherished me. He adored me.

He always had.

I kissed him and put my hand on his chest. Tom touched my face, and I thought about what it would be like. When the night finally arrived. When he could kiss me everywhere.

"You best be off," Jimmy said at last. "Don't want to miss your flight."

So we told him goodbye with the promise of our return. When we were home safe, I'd turn to Jimmy for moral support about the wedding. Jeanine would be my maid of honor. And Tom had already expressed an interest in having Eric as his best man.

That was something I never thought I'd hear him say. Now that Jeanine and Eric were back together, everything was perfect. I had no complaints. And we were going to Paris.

In the airport, it occurred to me that I'd never flown anywhere with Tom before. So many of the firsts in my life were with him. It felt special that we got to share another one.

"Ready?" Tom buckled his seatbelt.

"Yes." He'd given me the window seat. Even though I insisted he take it. So I kissed him with a smile. Then I looked out the window and did a double take. "Is it... snowing?"

Tom leaned over me. "Looks like it. I've never

seen snow before."

"Neither have I." I held his gaze. Another first.

"Do you think we'll have a white Christmas?" he asked.

"I hope so." I nuzzled his chest as we held hands.

Paris was eleven hours away. When we landed, it would be a new day.

* * *

When I woke up, it was morning. We had one stop-over in Atlanta. But I'd dozed back off as soon as I found my seat. Tom was still sleeping, as I got lost in a daydream.

What would it be like to wake up with him every morning? I'd never had a man like that. In my shower. In my bed. Well, naked in my bed. We'd slept together plenty of times.

It's just that sex had never been part of the equation.

I wondered why he was so passionate about waiting. Now that we had, I kind of worshipped him for that. He saw value in marriage and monogamy. He wanted me for a lifetime, not just one hot night. It was true—they didn't make men like this anymore.

I yawned and looked out my window. We were up in the clouds, flying way above the ocean. It felt strange to be coasting in the clear blue sky. Light as a feather. Like a bird.

I got up to use the restroom. Thankfully, there was no one inside. So I took my time in front of the mirror afterwards.

It had been a pleasant flight. No turbulence. No wind. No rain.

I'd finally gotten a glimpse of snow, but we'd left it in Georgia.

As I stared at my reflection, I wondered what Uncle Edmond would think of me. I ran my fingers through my hair and pinched my cheeks. I wasn't wearing much makeup, because it would have worn off in the night. And I honestly hadn't thought of it, since we were traveling.

The plane dipped as I slammed into the counter. I'd swallowed so much air that I couldn't breathe. And when the plane swerved again, I hit my head on the mirror.

I stumbled back and reached for something steady to hold on to. But then the lights flickered, and the plane shook until I landed on the floor. I put my head between my knees and held on for dear life. By some miracle, the lights came back on and I exhaled.

The pilot came on the intercom. Just mild turbulence. Nothing to worry about.

"Thank God." I tried to open the door, but the lock was jammed.

Before I had time to panic, the door flew open. And Tom was standing on the other side of it. Maybe it was the fear of dying in a plane crash. Or the stilted sense of euphoria.

For whatever reason, I grabbed his collar and pulled him into the bathroom. He shut the door and drew me into his arms. His eyes flew to the red mark on my head.

"Are you all right?" he asked.

"Yeah." I gave him a sexy smirk. "I'm much better now."

When the plane bucked, it sent Tom straight forward. He had me pinned to the sink. And I knew in that moment, that there was no place I'd rather be.

I ran my fingers through his hair and put my mouth on his. Tom wrapped his arms around my waist and lifted me onto the counter. Then we were kissing and gasping.

He trailed kisses down my neck. It felt like he was licking my wounds. He was making me whole. He was putting me back together again. And he hadn't even touched me yet.

I pushed against his chest and we slammed into the door. His hands tightened around my body, and I fell into him with bubbling laughter. He cradled my face in his hand.

It felt like the touch of an angel.

When his brown eyes burned amber, I bit his bottom lip. And he tasted my neck. We weren't usually like this. I couldn't describe it, but things were changing.

Maybe we weren't kids anymore.

The plane jerked forward with enough force to send us flying through the door. When I opened my eyes, Tom was lying on top of me. And passengers were staring at us. We were together on the floor with a hundred eyes on us, but I didn't care.

"My god!" One woman said. "Is that all you can think about?"

"It's not what it looks like." Tom burst into laughter. "I promise."

I covered my mouth and giggled. My cheeks were burning scarlet red.

"Oh look!" A school girl pointed at me. "They're engaged."

It was like a scene in a movie. The way everyone suddenly said aww...

I buried my face in his shirt. We couldn't stop laughing. Even with everyone staring.

Despite my embarrassment, there was no one I'd rather be found lying under in the middle of an airplane than Tom Sutton.

* * *

We landed in Paris around four. And I couldn't be happier.

Uncle Edmond sent a car for us, but we had to grab our luggage first. Even as we weaved our way through the airport, it hadn't sunk in yet. After all these years, I was finally getting to meet my family.

For so long, I'd felt out of place. And when I found out about the adoption, it confirmed a suspicion that had haunted me for a decade—that no one wanted me.

I leaned into Tom, and he looped his arm through mine. Last summer had been a little heaven and a lot of hell. But I'd gotten Jimmy out of it—a real father who loved me.

In a million years, I never would have imagined there to be more of them. But Uncle Edmond had two children—a son and a daughter. The first was married with a daughter. The second was a career woman, too invested in work for a husband or kids.

I mapped out a family tree in my mind. From the looks of it, they were my cousins. All of them. I'd never had a cousin before, or even a sibling for that matter.

A thrill raced through me. I was so excited to meet them. Especially Uncle Edmond's granddaughter, probably because we were the closest in age. She'd just turned sixteen.

"We landed a bit early," Tom said. "Do you want a bite to eat?"

"Yeah." My stomach rumbled at the thought. "Maybe a little something."

We picked out a cute little bistro, but the line was ridiculous. He volunteered to order the food, while I wandered into a gift shop across the way. I pretended to look around, but I was really watching Tom from afar. Even now, I loved everything about him.

The way he walked and talked. How he stood quietly in line, waiting his turn. He crossed his arms and looked up at the menu on the wall. Everything about this trip felt like a dream. And I wasn't planning on wasting a minute of it.

In the shop, I looked at a map of Paris. Then I bought a French-English dictionary. Neither of us spoke fluent French, so it might be handy during our stay. Maybe Uncle Edmond could teach me some clever phrases that would impress my American friends.

A man lingered at the edge of the gift shop. It took me a while to notice him, because I was so invested in finding the right dictionary. But when I did, it made my skin crawl.

He wore a business suit and a black hat. Looking back, I suppose there was nothing particularly odd about him. But he kept staring at a gift bag without really looking at it.

I had the feeling he wasn't genuinely shopping. And every time I moved, he seemed to take note. I bought the French-English dictionary, because I didn't want to feel paranoid. But on my way out of the shop, he bumped right into me.

"Sorry." I forced a smile. "I mean..." I flipped through the dictionary for a French translation.

"No." He straightened his jacket and took a step back. "Pardon me, Mademoiselle."

I stood stock still as he turned on his heel, disappearing into the airport. He was tall with dark hair. Something about him reminded me of Thin Man from Charlie's Angels.

"You okay?" Tom walked up with our food.

"Yeah." I grabbed a coffee from his hand.

"Who was that?" He put his arm around me, staring after the path he'd taken.

"I don't know." I took a sip of coffee and let it go.

"Well, do you want to eat?" he asked. "I don't think our ride will be here for about thirty minutes."

"Yeah." I nodded. "I'll call Edmond and let him know we've arrived."

Tom left to find us a table, but I kept staring into the crowd. The tall, thin stranger had disappeared into a sea of people. And there was something about him that I just couldn't put my finger on.

"So what do you think this castle is going to be like?" Tom took a bite of croissant.

"I don't know." I leaned back in my chair. "Well, I do actually."

Tom smiled. I was glad he hadn't said anything about my eating like a bird. But now that the moment was upon us, I just wasn't hungry. I was nervous.

In fact, I felt sick to my stomach.

"It should look something like this." I showed Tom a picture on my phone.

"Your uncle has invited us to stay there?" He lifted his brow in shock.

"Yeah. That's where we're headed."

Tom handed my phone back and put his food down. "What's up?"

"Nothing." I scooted forward and rubbed my arms. "I'm fine."

"You just seem a little..." He drank some

water. "...nervous."

"Well, I am nervous if I'm being perfectly honest." I twisted my hands under the table. "They've never met me before. What if they don't like me?"

"I wouldn't worry about that if I were you."

"But they live in a French castle. They're royalty. Uncle Edmond is a count."

"So?" Tom polished off my croissant.

"So, I'm just some ordinary girl from Savannah. There's nothing special about me."

He narrowed his eyes and smoldered. "That's the farthest thing from the truth."

I bowed my head, resting my cheek on my hand. Maybe it was exhaustion from the long flight—not to mention jetlag—but I felt like crying. I was tired and self-conscious. I can't really tell you why, because there was no particular reason for it. The feeling came out of nowhere and hit me like a ton of bricks. But that made it all the more potent.

"Addie." Tom grabbed my hand. "Come here."

"What?" I whined, shielding my eyes from his censure.

He pushed back in his chair and patted his lap. Since he kept pulling on my hand, I stood up and gave in to his strength. I lost my balance and sat down on his knee. And he circled his arms around my waist, drawing me into his warm body.

He kissed my cheek. "You are the most amazing girl I know."

I wrapped my arms around his neck and breathed him in. "Really?"

He nodded his head ever so slightly, but those amber eyes stayed on me. I leaned in, and he pressed his mouth to mine. It was a soft kiss, gentle enough to be friendly.

But I knew it meant more than that.

I put my head on his chest as he laced our fingers together. "I just want them to approve of me, you know? They're French nobility. And what if I'm not good enough?"

He lifted my chin, and I felt his breath on my face. "You're royalty, too."

"No, I'm not." I shook my head, pushing the thought away with the flick of my wrist.

"Yes, you are." He stared into my eyes, serious as a heart attack. "Maybe you don't see it now. But you will. And they're going to love you just as much as I do."

"You really think so?" My spirits lifted—a side effect of his sweet talking.

"Yeah, I do."

I caressed his cheek and then kissed him slowly. He buried his face in my neck and held me close, while I shut my eyes and took a breath. We stayed like that for the next ten minutes—just holding each other. And it was the greatest feeling in the world.

I'd just flown to the city of love with my new fiancé.

I had nothing to be worried about.

Chapter 9

When our driver arrived, my heart was beating a mile a minute. He was an older fellow with gentle manners and a sweet disposition. I hopped in the backseat with Tom as the driver stowed our luggage away in the trunk. His name was Fernand, and I liked him already.

"Do you think it will snow?" I asked.

"Oui," he chimed. "Tonight, it's very likely."

I leaned into Tom as he gazed out the window. The city was more beautiful and magnificent than I ever could have imagined. The sky was crystal clear, blue and pastel.

I put my head on his chest and closed my eyes. I wondered what Paris looked like at night—twinkling with lights. Maybe we could visit the Eiffel Tower then. There were so many sights I wanted to see during our trip. But for now, a quick tour would have to do.

Fernand pointed to landmarks on the drive. Some were familiar to me, some were like tasting candy for the first time. I wanted to pinch myself, because it didn't feel real.

But as the castle approached, I thought I might faint. My hands were clammy, and I couldn't breathe. So I leaned my head against the glass and then lay back on the seat.

"Hey." Tom squeezed my hand. "Are you okay?"

"Yeah," I inhaled. "Just a little nervous."

"I told you, you'll be fine." He wrapped his arm around my shoulder. "Come here."

So I nuzzled his chest and took a series of deep breaths. Fernand looked in the rearview mirror, and my cheeks flushed with embarrassment. But maybe that was good, because I'd turned white as a ghost.

"Fernand?" I was still having trouble breathing.

"Yes, mademoiselle." His white mustache curled up on either end.

"What is the count like?" I asked. "Can you tell me about him?"

"Very tall man," he started. "He's strict, always on time. He's been looking forward to meeting you."

"He has?" I said.

Why was it so hard for me to believe?

"Oui." He smiled in the mirror. "So has the rest of the family."

"Do you think you could keep talking?" I

asked. "I love your accent."

Flattered by my compliment, he carried on with the conversation. While I did love his accent, the way he spoke soothed me. So I closed my eyes and listened to every cadence.

"Why do you always do this?" Tom stroked my cheek. "Stop freaking out."

"I'm not freaking out." I kept my eyes closed.

"You're going to be fine." He slid his fingers between mine.

"I know." I looked up at him. "It's just—"

"Shh." He put his finger to my lips. "Stop talking."

For once, I listened. And it made the drive more comfortable. I squeezed Tom's hand and tried to relax, shutting my eyes again. Fernand's soothing voice lulled me to sleep. And before I knew it, we were driving through the open gate to my uncle's castle.

I wanted to say something. Anything would have been less rude. Tom had asked me a question, and Fernand was also waiting for a reply. But there were no words.

I put my hand on the glass and looked out the window. It was beyond my wildest dreams—like a castle from one of the many fairytales I'd read growing up. I stuck my finger out to count all the windows. If each one belonged to a room, then there must have been a hundred of them. It felt like a dream. I must have been imagining things.

"First impressions?" Tom whispered.

I stared at the castle in longing. "I don't belong in a place like this."

It was true. I wasn't a princess. I was an outsider, an American, an unwanted member of the family. For part of my life, I'd even thought I was an orphan. I didn't belong here.

"I can't do this." I moved to the middle of the backseat. "Fernand, please turn around and go back to the airport."

Fernand looked in the rearview mirror.

"No." Tom glared at me. "Fernand, keep driving."

"I don't want to do this," I said. "I don't belong here."

Tom grabbed my wrists. "We've flown all this way. I'm not gonna let you run now, just because you're scared."

There was a lump in my throat, as tears pooled in my eyes. "Fernand," I begged. "Please turn around. Take me back to the airport."

"No!" Tom applied more pressure. "We're not going anywhere. We're staying right here."

He looked deep into my eyes, pinning me to the backseat with that unruly gaze.

"Stop the car," I told Fernand. "Please, let me out."

Fernand pulled over on the side of the road. I opened the door and got out. We were already on the property, but only a few hundred yards past the main gate. It had already closed, which made my stomach somersault. So I sat down on the lawn and shivered.

"Addie." Tom got out of the car. "What are you doing?"

I pulled my knees into my chest and cried. There was no explanation for my tears. To be honest, I don't know why I'd picked that moment to have an emotional breakdown.

But my life had been filled with disappointment. People always letting me down. Family was something I'd yearned for desperately. And every time I got close, someone snatched it away. First with Daniel. Then Jimmy—luckily last summer he'd survived.

I was afraid to let these people in, because I would love them all.

And I didn't want to lose them.

"Baby." Tom sat down beside me. "Come here."

He put my head on his chest, and I didn't fight him. Then he ran his fingers through my hair, letting me get it all out. Whatever it was. He rubbed my back, and I wrapped my arms around him. He drew in a quick breath, because I'd been squeezing so tightly.

"It's okay," he coaxed. "Everything is going to be okay."

When I calmed down enough to stand, Tom helped me back to the car. I hated to think what must be going through Fernand's head. It made my cheeks turn scarlet.

As he helped me in, a tall man walked up to

the car. I'd heard gravel crunching but thought nothing of it in my hysteria. Now I realized, it must have been his footsteps.

"Well," the man said. "Am I ever going to meet my niece?"

I swallowed and swayed back. But Tom had his arm around me, keeping me centered.

"Uncle Edmond?" I stared at him in awe.

"Yes." He approached us. "Who else would it be?"

I recognized him from the photos I'd seen online. But he'd changed since they were taken. He had a white beard. And what was left of his hair was gray—closer to salt than pepper. Fernand was right. Edmond was a tall man, but he had the best smile.

"Hi." I gave a small wave. And then Tom gave me a little push.

"I'm not the big bad wolf," Edmond joked. "I don't bite."

Letting out a giggle, I took another step forward until he pulled me into his arms. In a matter of seconds, I was crying again. When Edmond noticed, he patted me on the back.

"No need to cry, dear. Fernand, were you having trouble with the car?" he asked.

"No." I spoke up before Fernand got punished for my procrastination.

"Well then." Fernand helped me into the car. "Why don't we go inside?"

I couldn't believe Edmond had been so

PEARL WHITE

impatient to meet me that he'd walked the long drive to the front gate. Tom sat down beside me as Fernand drove us up to the estate. And Edmond entertained us with tall tales he'd heard from his ancestors about the castle.

When Fernand parked, I let Tom open my door. There was an enchanting water fountain just by the drive, and many more on the grounds. Edmond mentioned a rose garden as Tom helped Fernand with our luggage. Apparently, it was a place where Antoinette had spent a lot of time in her youth. I couldn't wait to discover it.

Edmond introduced us to the staff in the foyer. There was a butler, an assistant and a pair of maids. He had fewer servants than I'd anticipated. But this pleased me a great deal.

On the way to our rooms, I couldn't stop craning my neck. I'd never seen such high ceilings in a house before. The floors were made of marble. And the place was flowing with curated art. Some of the finest oil paintings I'd ever seen. And family portraits, of course.

Cosette—Edmond's assistant, who I'd spoken to over the phone—showed us to our rooms. She was in her late twenties with chestnut hair and a slim figure. I'd read online that Edmond was a widower. His wife had died of cancer a decade ago, and I was sad to hear it. I'm sure it was a touchy subject, so I had no intentions of bringing it up.

"Do you like it?" Cosette led me into an

elegant bedroom.

It must have been at least a thousand square feet. There was lounge furniture and a fireplace, even a glass chandelier that hung overhead. Bay windows looked over the back of the castle. I took my scarf off and sat down by the window, shaking my head in awe.

"Well?" Cosette asked.

When I looked back at her, she was smiling. Since I'd arrived, everyone seemed so amused by my reaction to seeing the castle for the first time. I was utterly speechless.

I didn't say anything, because I couldn't find the words.

"I'll leave you to get settled." Cosette closed the French doors on her way out.

I walked around the guest room. Everything about the place screamed high class and good breeding. The bureau had been polished to shine. And the antique furniture looked too nice for me to sit on. So I ambled over to the elegant king size bed and lay down.

Even the ceiling looked exquisite. There was a mural of baby angels floating in the clouds. They looked cherubic. Chubby smiles and rolls of baby fat juxtaposed with ethereal wings and golden curls. Some of them had a bow and arrow. Like Cupid.

I leaned my head back and laughed. Because it felt like a dream.

When someone knocked on the door, I

straightened up. "You can come in."

Tom walked in and left the door cracked behind him. "Wow. Look at this place."

"I know, right?" I sat up on my hands. "I can't believe my grandmother grew up in a place like this. Why would she ever leave?"

"Daniel." Tom slipped his hands in his pockets and approached the bed.

"Yeah." I smiled at the expensive quilt beneath me. "I guess you're right."

"Do you have room for one more?" he asked.

"Of course." I patted the empty space beside me.

He lay down and looked up at the ceiling. "Now that's not in my room."

I broke into uproarious laughter—the kind that took a lot of effort to stop. Then I looked at him and turned his face towards me. He kissed my forehead and caressed my hand. Then his arm went around my back, and I rested my head on his shoulder.

"I know this trip was all about me, but I really appreciate you coming along."

"I don't mind." He stroked my arm. "I know how happy this makes you."

I nuzzled his chest and shut my eyes, running my hand down the side of his torso.

"I can't believe we're here." I let out a breath. "Finally, after all this time."

He picked up my hand and looked at the engagement ring he'd given me. Then he ran his thumb over the diamond and laced his fingers through mine. I kissed him and buried my face in the crook of his neck.

Everything about today had been amazing.

But it would've meant nothing without him here.

* * *

We fell asleep in my bed for an hour. But I hoped no one at the castle got the wrong idea. Tom was my fiancé. And we were in modern day Paris—the city of love.

We weren't doing anything scandalous. But at our age, most teenagers already had. I hoped rather than believed that they wouldn't hold an assumption like that against us.

Dinner would be served in half an hour. So Tom went back to his room to shower and change. I slipped into the private bathroom attached to my suite and my jaw dropped.

There was art on the walls and a garden tub fit for a queen. Despite being pressed for time, I indulged in a bubble bath before getting dressed for the evening. No one had warned me of a dress code for dinner, so I assumed jeans and a nice sweater would be fine.

I put on a little bit of makeup and let my hair down. Then I put on my newest pair of leather boots in the hope of looking a bit dressier. There was a bottle of perfume in the bathroom, so I dabbed some on my neck and wrists. It smelled delightful—like spring.

When I left my room, Tom was waiting for me in the hallway. He looked fresh from his shower and smelled like pine. He took my hand and we kissed, ready to brave the world of French aristocracy.

"Addie?" A man approached me in the hall. One I'd never seen before.

"Yes." I tilted my head to the side and looked him up and down.

"I'm Ashton." He extended a large hand. "Edmond's eldest."

"Oh, hi." I gave him a hug. "It's nice to meet you. So you're my..."

"Your mother is my first cousin," he said. "That makes us cousins as well."

"That's right." I'd been staring at his eyes since I saw him. It was almost impossible for me to look away. "This is Tom, my fiancé."

They shook hands and exchanged casual conversation. I couldn't stop staring at Ashton. He was extremely tall like his father. But the resemblance stopped there.

He had dirty blonde hair, the kind that darkens in time. I put him between thirty and forty, since Edmond married later in life. I'd read that his wife had been much younger, so that added up. But something about Ashton was mesmerizing.

"Are you all right?" He'd caught me staring.

"Yes. Just not sure which way the dining room is," I said.

"Downstairs." He put his arm out. "I'll escort you."

"Okay." I took his arm and looked back at Tom.

He snickered behind us on the staircase. We weren't used to such formalities at dinner time. And I tried not to panic over whether or not we were underdressed.

"You're from Georgia?" Ashton asked.

"Yes. Savannah." I observed the castle as we walked.

"And it's your first time in Europe?" he wondered.

"Yes," I said. "How could you tell?"

"You seem a little bit..." he hesitated "nervous."

"That's because I am," I confessed.

"Why?" He lowered his voice. "Your fiancé?"

"No." I furrowed my brow. "Why would you think that?"

"I thought it might be amour fou."

"What?" I leaned my head back to look at him.

"You've never heard of that before?"

"No. What is it?"

"You might call it passion—a kind of mad love."

"Well, we are crazy about each other," I said. "So there's no denying that."

"That's what I thought." Ashton turned a corner as I walked with him.

"Do you know about my mother?" I asked.

"Not much. Papa doesn't like us talking about her."

"Oh." I spotted the dining room straight ahead.

"But I'm sorry for your loss."

There were two women waiting by the dining room table. And Ashton rushed to greet them both. He kissed the first and hugged the second, while I reached out for Tom.

"Addie, allow me to introduce my wife, Juliette."

"It's very nice to meet you." I shook her hand.

She was average height with bright blue eyes and waves of raven black hair. I knew nothing about her, but when she smiled it dimpled her cheeks. I thought Juliette and Ashton looked lovely together. Their daughter was an obvious combination of the two.

"This is Adeline," Juliette said. "She just turned sixteen."

"Uncle Edmond told me," I smiled.

Adeline pulled me into her arms and gave me a big hug. I'd never been a touch-me-not, so I thought it was remarkably sweet. I'd just arrived at the castle, but I already had a fan.

"I've been looking forward to your arrival," Adeline said.

"I'd be lying if I said I hadn't been counting down the days, too." I felt Tom behind me and wanted to punish myself for forgetting him. "Oh.

Let me introduce you to my fiancé." I pushed him in front of me and looped my arm through his. "Tom Sutton."

After pleasant conversation, everyone took a seat in the dining room. Uncle Edmond arrived last and sat at the head of the table. He seemed angry about something, and I hoped Tom and I weren't underdressed. We were the only ones at dinner wearing jeans. But no one had informed me of a dress code. How was I to know basic castle attire?

"Where is your daughter?" I asked.

We breezed through the first three courses, and I hoped dessert was coming next. I wasn't sure if I had the stomach to hold any more food. And I didn't want to miss the best part.

"I assume you're speaking of Genevieve," Edmond grumbled. "Well, she'll show her face when she gets good and damn ready. I never have been able to control her."

The table fell in silence, while I looked at Tom.

"Genevieve is a little stubborn sometimes," Ashton said.

"Stubborn?" Edmond gulped red wine. "That's not what I'd call it."

"Will she be joining us for dinner?" I wondered.

Edmond threw his napkin on the table. "I wouldn't bet on it."

He stood up and marched out of the room.

Even though he traveled all the way upstairs, I still heard a door slam thirty seconds later. It made me flinch.

"Don't worry about that," Ashton said. "Genevieve has always been selfish."

"What does she do for a living?" I drummed my fingers on the table.

"She's an art dealer," he said. "That's our connection to Louvre."

"Did she arrange the ceremony? For the necklace, I mean?" I asked.

"Yeah. It's in a few days. We're all supposed to be there."

Crème brûlée arrived for dessert. It couldn't have come at a better time.

I took a small bite of the delicious custard. In eighteen years, I'd never tried it before. Even with Tom for a live-in chef. It was a delightful treat. Especially while in France.

I studied Ashton like a work of art. Now that Edmond had stormed off, he was the only man left at the table who was my flesh and blood. I'd never been around someone who shared my physical features. Growing up, my adoptive parents looked nothing like me.

For the longest time, I'd thought I didn't look like anyone.

Ashton caught me staring and gave a small smile. I could see a resemblance to Antoinette. Even though, to Ashton, she'd been an aunt.

It was crazy to think I had so much in common

LINDSAY MARIE MILLER

with a relative stranger. But we shared the same bloodline. And it bonded me to him in a way nothing else could.

For the rest of my stay, I'd be haunted by what we shared.

His eyes looked just like mine.

Chapter 10

After dinner, Adeline gave me a tour of the castle. She was clever and pretty, but helplessly shy. Her hair was as dark as her mother's. And her eyes looked like the sky.

Despite her bashfulness, we became fast friends in a matter of hours. She poured her heart out to me in a room dedicated to the family lineage. It was filled with portraits.

Adeline didn't have many friends at school. They teased her and left her out of anything involving a group. Her one constant had been a beau she wouldn't name. But he'd dumped her before the holidays. He'd been her first boyfriend, so she was crushed.

I wanted to give her advice. Let her know that things would get better from here. But how could I say that? I'd never suffered heartache before. Not in the form of a break-up.

Absent parents on the other hand? Now, I had that agony down to a science.

"How did you and Tom meet?" Adeline asked.

"At school." I winced, because that would only remind her of her ex. "Actually, we're neighbors. We both live in the country on a couple hundred acres. He's not right next door. Not literally, but he's the closest neighbor I have."

"And how did you know?" She sat down in a velvet chair. "That he was the one?"

"Well, I didn't at first." I took the seat beside her. "It's happened over time."

"How long have you been together?" she asked.

"We met almost a year ago. But we were friends first. For a little bit."

"May I see your ring?" She eyed the white diamond on my finger.

So I held out my hand and let her look at it. "It was my grandmother's."

"It's beautiful," she said wistfully. "I'm happy for you."

"Thanks." I blushed at her words.

"When is the wedding?" she asked. "Have you set a date?"

"Not yet." It was the question everyone had been asking. "But we're still in high school, so we have plenty of time. Maybe in the spring or next summer after we graduate."

She nodded and got up. I watched her circle

the room, since I was too tired to follow her. She stared at a portrait of Edmond. He looked so young, maybe in his early twenties.

"My grandfather can be very cruel sometimes. I'm sorry about what he said at dinner tonight." She admired his painting with scrutiny—an at a distance kind of love.

"You mean about Genevieve?" I said. "That's all right. I'm only a guest."

"I love Aunt Genevieve. But they've never seen eye to eye."

"I'll keep that in mind." I tucked the kernel of truth away for later.

"You know, there are legends about this place," Adeline said. "They say a young widow died here. Her husband was killed in battle. When she heard he was dead, she put on her wedding dress and jumped off the banister. They say her ghost walks the halls at night."

I wrapped my arms around my waist and shivered.

"I could never live here year round," she said. "I'm too scared of this place."

"Is her portrait in this room?"

"Yeah, I think so." Adeline furrowed her brow until she'd spotted it. "That one."

I walked over to the portrait, while Adeline fed me backstory. But I didn't hear a word she said. My pulse was hammering too loudly in my ears to understand her.

The lady in the painting was stunning. Black

hair. Ivory skin. Green eyes.

She had softer features than Antoinette. A heart-shaped face and pouty lips.

She was wearing a white dress. Wedding white. So it must have been her wedding dress.

"That's the woman who killed herself?" I asked.

"Yeah." Adeline looked at the portrait. "That's what they say."

I took a step back. I felt light-headed, like I couldn't breathe.

It might have been my imagination. But it felt like the war widow was staring right at me.

Her emerald eyes pierced my soul like a dagger. That didn't freak me out.

The dress she wore looked just like Antoinette's. That didn't freak me out.

The source of my fear lay at the base of her throat.

She was wearing the necklace.

Someone knocked on the door and I jumped. It was only Ashton, but I'd caught my breath just the same. I turned to Adeline, and she looked just as startled as me.

"Didn't mean to frighten you, girls," he said. "But it's snowing outside."

"Oh, it is!" Adeline leapt up. You'd have thought she'd never had a white Christmas before. "Come on, Addie." She grabbed my hand and dragged me out of the room.

Together, we ran down the staircase and found

Tom in the den. He smiled when he saw me, and I gave him a quick kiss. Adeline stood by the window and watched it snow.

Ashton walked into the den with Juliette on his arm. And I was happy to see them. Edmond must have retired for the night, because he was nowhere to be seen.

For the next hour, we drank hot chocolate and sat by the fire. Ashton recounted old stories about the family from Christmases past. I'd just arrived, but it already felt like I'd missed so much. Even now, I didn't know if I'd ever be able to catch up.

"Adeline told me there was a ghost in the castle," I said.

"Oh, I wouldn't worry about that." Ashton lowered his voice. "The only ghost you need to fear is the man upstairs." He pointed at the ceiling.

"You mean..." I thought he was talking about God.

"Papa," Ashton chuckled. "Why? Who did you think I was talking about?"

We laughed, as I got the feeling Ashton liked to tease him.

"My mother passed away around this time of year. It's always hard on him."

"Oh." That explained the count's behavior. "I'm sorry to hear that."

"Yeah, me too." Ashton drank his hot chocolate, while the room fell in silence.

"Well, it's getting late," I said. "I better get ready for bed."

"Yes." Juliette stood to give me a hug. "I'm sure you've had a long day."

I told everyone good night and Tom walked me to my room. Now that we were engaged, I thought about sex on a daily basis. It was hard to part ways as he returned to his room. All the way down the hall. Right now, I'd love nothing more than to curl up under the covers with him. But that time would come. And I was looking forward to it.

After slipping into flannel pajamas, I locked the door to my bedroom. I knew the story Adeline told me was just a tall tale. But I wanted to be careful, just in case.

I got in bed and turned out the light. Then I tucked myself in and stared at the mural of cherubs on the ceiling. I closed my eyes with a smile, thinking of the morning snow.

It was my first night in a French castle. And I'd never felt more at home.

* * *

The next morning I woke to a desert of snow. I'd never seen anything like it. I dressed in warm layers and knocked on Tom's door. But he wanted to sleep longer, so I headed outside without him.

Adeline was already there building a snowman with her dad. I ran across the back yard and watched my breath. It was such a drastic change from Savannah, but I loved it.

We spent the better part of the morning in a

snowball fight. Then I wandered into the woods with Adeline. A river ran through the wilderness, and it had begun the process of freezing over. Adeline hoped we'd be able to ice skate tomorrow. I'd never been.

Juliette made cinnamon rolls for breakfast. They were the most delicious treats I'd ever tasted. I couldn't remember a single time Eleanor had cooked breakfast. It wasn't in her.

When Tom came downstairs, I kissed him on the cheek. But he was grumpy and uncharacteristically bashful. Maybe he wasn't used to company, but it wasn't like they were strangers. We were with family. My family. And I was loving every minute of it.

Uncle Edmond left to handle business—whatever that meant. I expected Ashton to leave with him, since they were in the same industry. But my cousin wanted to enjoy his vacation. He said Edmond was a workaholic. And right now, he needed a distraction.

Adeline invited me to go Christmas shopping with her parents. I ran the idea by Tom. Let's just say, he didn't jump at the idea of shopping. But he came anyway.

As we tried on clothes, I got the feeling that Tom was miserable. Adeline reminded me of Jeanine, so our shopping spree quickly turned into a girl's trip. But Ashton was a man, and he didn't seem to mind. He even bought me a 7-day wardrobe for my stay at the castle.

No matter how much I denied him, Ashton insisted. So he spent an obscene fortune on clothes and shoes. I felt guilty, but he just wouldn't take no for an answer.

On the drive home, Tom wasn't saying much. I knew he didn't like Ashton taking care of me. To be honest, I still had a credit card attached to Jeffrey and Eleanor. But I'd never been a vindictive person. I wasn't going to blow their life savings on a revenge splurge in Paris.

Regardless, it all rubbed Tom the wrong way. He turned in early that night, while I stayed up watching Christmas movies with Adeline. Uncle Edmond had already gone to bed. But at least he'd talked to us for a good hour before he headed upstairs.

I meant to have a private word with Tom. But the next day, Ashton announced the itinerary bright and early. He was taking us on a guided tour of Paris. I'd never been so excited. Adeline was jumping up and down, even though she'd seen it all before.

So we strolled the streets of Paris until noon. And then Ashton took us to a chic restaurant for lunch. The menu may have been in French, but I knew a high priced entrée when I saw one.

Tom offered to pay for the two of us. But Ashton shut him down. I thanked my cousin for his generosity—something I hadn't stopped doing since he'd purchased my elaborate wardrobe. But Tom looked out the window with a sneer. We needed to talk.

After the meal, my family headed outside to look around. I went to the bathroom on the pretense of fixing my makeup. But Tom caught my drift. I'd never been a glamour girl. So I stood in the empty bathroom and waited until he finally knocked on the door.

"Hey." I let him in and locked the door behind us.

Tom looked around the bathroom and frowned. He had his hands in his pockets, and I hadn't seen him crack a smile all day. I couldn't figure out what was wrong with him.

"Why have you been acting so strange?" I asked point blank.

"I'm not acting strange," he said.

"Well, you're not acting like yourself." I put my hands on my hips.

He waited a long while before he spoke again. "I don't think it's right for them to be spending all this money on you. You just met them. I don't like him footing the bill."

"I never asked him to. Ashton is the one who brought it up."

"And you sure didn't stop him," he said. "How much did that dress cost?"

"Uncle Edmond said I needed something for the commemoration at Louvre. And Juliette is the one who picked it out. They're French. They live here. I trust them."

He rocked back on his heels. "They're gaining

control over you."

"What? No, they're not. Ashton is just being nice."

"That's what you think. I've thought people were family before too, you know," he argued.

I knew he was referring to Daniel. It had all been a lie. He was my grandfather, not his.

"What are you saying?" I asked.

He moistened his lips and grabbed my hand. "You've trusted them so easily."

"They're my family, Tom!" I yelled. "What am I supposed to do?"

"Well, where have they been all this time? I've been here, I've..."

I touched his face. "Please don't do this. Not now. Not when I'm finally—"

"What?" A furrow formed between his brows.

"Happy," I said.

He removed my hand from his face. "But not happy with me?"

"Tom, I didn't say that. This is different."

"How?" he smoldered. "How is it any different?"

"You're my love." I grabbed his face in my hands. "But they're my family."

He let out a breath and stared at the ground.

"Please. Don't make me choose between you."

He pressed his forehead to mine. "I just want you to know that you'll be taken care of. I can't buy you thousand dollar dresses every day. But I will take care of you, Addie."

"I never asked you to."

He pulled away and walked towards the door.

"Just let me get through this trip. I don't know how long it will be before I can come back to Paris again. Once I start college..."

"You mean, once you marry me." He watched me, and I felt like crying.

"I just want to spend this time with them while I can," I said.

"I know." He nodded. "Carpe diem, right?"

"Right." It took all I could not to cry.

He walked out of the bathroom. I hardly remember the guided tour that followed.

* * *

The commemoration at Louvre was the day after tomorrow. So Genevieve stopped by to help us with the preparations. She looked like her brother, except she had darker hair. And I was pleased that she could give us some tips for the ceremony. I was really nervous.

Adeline and I modeled our gowns for Edmond in his office. I could tell he wanted everything to be perfect, because he was particular about the slightest detail. Even his beef with Genevieve seemed to be on the backburner for now.

Adeline looked elegant in red satin. And her gown flowed down her long legs in stride. I wore a green satin gown her mother had picked out for me. Even Genevieve agreed that emerald was perfect, because it would bring out my eyes.

When Edmond was satisfied, he asked Adeline to leave. Genevieve shut the door and slid a black briefcase on the table. I felt nervous about the ceremony already and kept practicing my walk. It was hard to move in the silver heels Juliette was letting me borrow.

"Addison, come." Edmond waved me over to his desk. "Your grandmother and I shared a special bond. And I've missed her for many years."

Genevieve opened the briefcase. The emerald necklace was inside.

"I've asked Adeline to leave, because I didn't want to hurt her feelings." He turned the briefcase towards him. "But I was wondering if you would like to wear the necklace one last time?"

I looked at Genevieve. "Go on," she said.

"It's over a hundred carats." Edmond picked up the necklace and laid the stone against my sternum. "And I think nothing would make my sister happier than for you to wear it." He clasped the latch at the back, while I approached a hanging mirror nearby.

I stared at my reflection and touched the necklace. It would always be the most enchanting piece of jewelry to ever catch my eye. I was sad to see it go, but my life was worth more than a gemstone. Because I planned on living the rest of it with Tom.

"How much is it worth?" I'd always assumed millions. But I'd never known.

"It's no diamond, sweetheart," Genevieve said. "But based on the cut and clarity alone, I could get a million out of it. And I could get a whole lot more based on what's inside."

I furrowed my brow and frowned at my reflection. Edmond shot Genevieve a deathly glare, and I could see how they didn't see eye to eye. When he took the necklace off me, I watched Antoinette's legacy get locked up in a black leather briefcase.

"Should I tell her?" Genevieve eyed her father and he nodded.

"Tell me what?" I asked.

"We were thinking of letting you wear it."

"At the commemoration ceremony?" I asked.

"Just in the morning," Edmond grumbled. "We'll have plenty of security and protection for you. But if you don't want to wear it, I understand. It was just a thought."

"No." I beamed at the thought. "I'd love to."

"Great." Genevieve shut the briefcase. "It's all settled then." She kissed Edmond on the cheek and turned to leave. "I'm having it cleaned tomorrow. It will be good as new."

Once she left, I looked at Edmond. "Thank you. For everything."

"It's my Christmas gift to you." He kissed my forehead as we walked out.

On my way upstairs, I couldn't believe what was happening. I was living in a fairytale. And I felt like a true guest of honor.

They'd invited me to be the belle of the ball.
How could I say no?

Chapter 11

From my bedroom, the castle grounds looked like a winter wonderland. Treetops were covered in snow, like a baker had dipped them in cream. I'd never seen anything like it.

I took a seat on the comfy window bench, decked out with plush pillows. Then I leaned against the glass, nursing a cup of hot tea. What it must be like to live in the lap of luxury.

It was the eve of the commemoration, and I'd been thinking about my grandmother. The way my future and her past were so inexplicably intertwined.

As my mind wandered, I had a scary thought. If Antoinette had stayed in France, I would have been here all along. Surely, she would have married a comparable royal. And then I would have descended from pure blue bloods. But maybe I had it all wrong.

With Antoinette in France, I wouldn't have been born at all.

I pressed my hand to the glass. It felt cool to the touch, so I blew warm air on my handprint. I'll bet Antoinette had sat right here, in this very room, daydreaming about my grandfather. When she fled Paris to be with him, she had quite literally saved me.

"Knock. Knock." Tom stood in the doorway. He was watching me.

"Come in." I set my tea down as he walked over. "Sit down."

He sat in front of me and turned towards the window. "It's a beautiful night."

"Yeah, I'm starting to think it's like this every night," I smiled.

We'd been here a total of three days, and I'd already made up my mind.

Everything about this place was elegant. Even the snow fell gracefully. I'd been victim to the castle's charms from the moment we arrived. Now, I didn't know how I'd ever go back.

"Are you okay?" he asked.

I looked up in surprise. Things had been weird between us. But today had been a good day. Hopefully a sign of better days to come. I didn't want any more bad blood between us.

"It's like you're under a spell or something." He waved his hand in front of my face.

"Stop." I closed my hand over his. "I'm not under a spell."

"Then what is it?" His fingertips grazed my palm. "It feels like we've hardly seen each other since we got here."

I shut my eyes and sighed. I wished I could say that nothing was farther from the truth.

Since our argument in the restaurant bathroom, I'd been keeping him at a distance. Today had been great, because I'd been going off with my family every chance I could get. Selfishly, I'd left Tom out. But I wanted to enjoy my time here with relatives.

In fact, I was so desperate for a family, that I'd forgotten his deepest secret.

I was his.

I dropped his hand and leaned against the pillows. Then I looked out the window and picked up my tea. It was still warm, cooled to just the right temperature. It was perfect.

Tom took the tea cup away from me. And I shot him a displeasing look.

"I feel like you're pulling away from me," he said.

Usually, I would have spouted off in anger. But being in Europe had calmed me. Softened me around the edges. Like now, when I was wound too tight.

I looked to see if the door was closed. And it was. He must have shut it on the way inside—a detail I'd failed to notice. He wanted privacy in the castle. A moment between us.

I gazed into his eyes and caressed his cheek.

He circled his hand around my wrist, ensuring physical contact. It wasn't enough if I touched him. He had to touch me, too.

There was so much love in his heart. He had mountains to give. And I was scalding with the same desire he kept stowed away. So hot, it burned just to think about.

I leaned into his kiss. And it was a sweet one.

Soft in the beginning, like the first time we kissed. Even now, I shivered when he touched me. And then I melted beneath his love, lost in tingly, prickly, electric emotion.

His arm snaked around my back, as I slid into his body. I ran my fingers through his hair and met him chest to chest. He teased my lower lip, breathing faster and faster.

I felt how much he wanted me. Just from his kiss alone. So I slowed down and put my head on his chest, lying on top of him. He held me there by the window, cradled in his arms. And I closed my eyes when he started petting my hair.

"I wish we were married already," I grumbled.

He put his hand on my back. "You do?"

"Yeah," I yawned, nuzzling his torso. "Don't you?"

He sat up. "Open your eyes."

I peeled my eyelids back with a grouchy groan. "What is it?"

"Come here." He got off the bench. "There's something I want to show you."

He took my hand and we left my bedroom.

Then he led me down the hall and into his. I looked over my shoulder to make sure no one saw us. We weren't in the eighteenth century, but they were old-fashioned around here. And we'd been placed in separate bedrooms for a reason. So whatever we were doing, we better not get caught.

Tom must have been on the same wavelength, because he closed the door behind us. Then he opened up the French doors leading out to the balcony. It was covered in snow.

I took a breath, and it showed in the air. "I can't believe it's real."

Tom pulled me into his side, while I admired the view. The front of the castle had just as much snow. But all of the water fountains were frozen. I thought they were exquisite.

Everyone here had respect for the fine arts. I loved it. Because when I learned to draw, all Eleanor would ever do is frown. In Europe, they saw value in human expression.

I didn't know if I'd ever find a like-minded culture anywhere else.

"I love it here," I said. "It makes me feel close to her."

"To your grandmother?" he asked. I felt his eyes on me.

"Yes. Can you imagine what it must have been like to grow up here?" I pulled the sleeves down on my sweater and leaned over the balcony. "For the first time in my life, I finally feel like I'm in a place where I belong, where I'm loved and wanted."

"But Savannah is home," Tom said.

"No." I caught a snowflake in my palm. "It's never felt like home to me."

He furrowed his brow. But when he opened his mouth, no words came out.

"When I met you, I was miserable," I confessed. "You were the first thing that felt like home. But you made me feel safe. The only home I'll ever need is in your arms."

"But you like it here," he said. "I can tell. You're happy."

"I am happy." I touched his hand. "But it's because I'm here with you."

It was true. Despite our disagreements, I'd miss him if he were gone.

He leaned over the balcony with me. And we stood like that. Peaceful and quiet. Watching the snow. Until he rubbed my shoulder and turned me towards him.

"What if..." He hung on my every glance.

I searched his eyes. "What if... what?" I giggled

"What if we got married here?"

I furrowed my brow.

"I mean, you just said you love it here. And your family is already here."

"When?" I looked for affirmation. "Now?"

"In a few days, maybe. Would that give you enough time?"

"You want to get married this week? But Tom, it's Christmas."

PEARL WHITE

"I know it's Christmas." He grabbed my hands. "That's what makes it perfect."

"I don't know." It was so sudden, it scared me. "I haven't even had time to plan. And what will Uncle Edmond think? We just show up and spring a wedding on him?"

Tom grinned ear to ear.

"What?" I asked.

"I already told him, and he'd love to have the wedding here."

I turned away and touched the railing. I needed the snow to cool down.

"He knows someone who can handle all the legal stuff, the paperwork. And we could have a short honeymoon afterwards. We're already in Europe. We could fly to—"

"You did all of this behind my back?" I accused. "Without even asking me first?"

"It was supposed to be a surprise. But I had to tell you something before we—"

"How can you spring a wedding on me like this? Right before Christmas! You know how important it is for me to be here with my family. And now you're trying to hijack the whole trip!"

"Addie, calm down. I'm not hijacking anything."

I'd been so convinced I was a new person in Paris. But look at me. I had a quick temper. One that couldn't be suppressed by a six hour time difference and a little snow.

"It just feels so rushed." I explained. "I don't

want to feel rushed."

"Okay, baby. I'm sorry. We won't. I'm not trying to rush you."

I looked up at him and moaned, "But I do want to marry you."

He looked confused. Like I'd given him whiplash.

"I guess I just don't know if I'm ready. I feel so confused."

"Hey." He rubbed my cheek. "It's normal to get cold feet before the wedding."

"I don't have cold feet, Tom. I want to marry you."

"Then what is it?" He was so patient with me, he deserved an Oscar.

"I just want to make sure we do it right. Everything is happening so fast. Is it the right time? I'm waiting for the moment to feel... I don't know, something. But I just..."

"I know it's scary." He cradled my face in his hands. "But sometimes the best things in life come with a little fear. That doesn't mean it won't be great."

"I know, I know. I just thought when I got to this point in my life, it would feel different." It never occurred to me that it would happen so fast.

"How are you wanting it to feel?" he asked.

"Like it does in the movies."

"But it does feel like the movies," he said. "We're just not acting."

I stood on the balcony as he walked away.

Then I hugged myself, feeling like a witch. How did I always end up hurting him, when I was just trying to express how I felt?

* * *

There was a knock on my door in the morning. I needed to be up early for the commemoration ceremony. But I'd tossed and turned and hardly slept all night.

I put on a silk robe Adeline had given me and opened the door. Genevieve marched into the room like a woman on a mission—already dressed for the occasion. She put the leather briefcase down on the card table by the couch and went into my closet.

As she marched around my room, I stood there yawning and bleary-eyed. It would feel so good to crawl back into bed where it was nice and warm for just a little while longer.

But in the blink of an eye, Genevieve had a hair and make-up crew dragging me into the bathroom. One of them pushed me into a chair in front of the mirror. I looked tired and cranky, which I was. But when Genevieve handed me a cup of coffee, all was well.

I sat in that chair for two hours while the beauty crew primped and preened. I'll admit—it was nice being pampered. But I'd rather have the extra two hours of sleep.

When they were done, I stood up and looked at my reflection. I may have felt lousy, but I looked flawless. My makeup was fresh and immaculate—just like the movie stars. I boasted a bold smoky eye and smoldering bronzer. My lashes had never been this long.

I was eighteen years old. But they'd made me look twenty-five.

My hair was styled in a messy French twist. And despite the pile of locks on my head, it actually felt comfortable. I lifted a hand to touch it, but the stylist slapped it away.

They covered me in hairspray and perfume. I couldn't wait to return and take a long hot bath. I'd been coughing for the last ten minutes from the fumes.

My nails were last. I suggested a French manicure, but no one caught my joke. The makeup artist chose metallic green instead. And it was the exact shade of the necklace.

Once my toenails dried, a fashionista helped me into my gown. It dragged the ground until I put on Juliette's silver wedges. There was a slit up the thigh and a deep V that showed some cleavage. But Genevieve looked pleased as she opened the briefcase.

The makeup artist gave me deep red glitter lips. And I hoped that was the final touch.

I stayed in front of the mirror, as Genevieve put the necklace on me. She fastened the clasp at the nape of my neck and took a step back. I waited for her to say something.

"How does it feel?" she asked.

Realizing she meant the necklace, I said, "Cold."

She laughed and went into the closet. Then she opened a big box on my bed. There was a white mink coat inside. And she'd ordered a second for Adeline as well.

"Won't you be the talk of Paris?" She squeezed my arm in front of the mirror.

The beauty crew left and Genevieve followed them out. My stomach was rumbling since I'd had coffee for breakfast. But there was no time now. Genevieve said the car would be arriving in less than thirty minutes. And I couldn't possibly eat like this anyway.

I heard footsteps and saw Tom in the mirror. He was wearing a tuxedo, and his hair was slicked back with gel. When he walked into the room, I felt naked and vulnerable.

He looked at me and put his hand on his chest. "Wow."

"Really? You don't think it's too much, because I feel like—"

He kissed my hand and scanned my figure. "No, not at all."

I swallowed and eyed my reflection one last time. In addition to the necklace, I was wearing a pair of diamond earrings Genevieve had given me. And the engagement ring.

Tom wrapped his hands around my stomach and looked at us in the mirror. He rested his chin on my bare shoulder, and I felt shivers tingle down my spine. One day, our wedding night would come. And his touch alone would be the death of me.

"Doesn't she look gorgeous?" Genevieve reentered the room.

"Yes." Tom pulled away but kept holding my hand.

"You two will need to be downstairs in ten minutes. We have the car ready."

"Already?" I asked.

"Yes, darling. You're the queen today," she chimed, leaving again.

"What about the necklace?" Tom asked.

"What about it?" I shot him an odd look.

"You're not actually going to wear it to the museum. Are you?"

"Yes. As a token of gratitude and respect for Antoinette. My grandmother," I stressed. "In case you've forgotten. That's why we're here, remember?"

Tom walked across the room and shut the door. He wasn't going to budge on this.

"Take it off," he said.

"Excuse me?" I glared at him. "You don't get to tell me what to do."

"When you're putting yourself in danger, yes I do. Now take it off."

"No," I growled. "This is the last chance I may ever have to wear my grandmother's necklace. And I'm not taking it off. Unless you pry it away from my dead body."

"After everything we've been through, I can't believe you'd do something so stupid."

"Tom, Edmond asked me to wear it today. I'm the last heir to the necklace."

"Then why are you letting him tell you what to do with it?" he asked.

"Because he's invited me to stay in his castle for Christmas. And I already told him I didn't want it. I'm glad we're donating it to Louvre. Where it can finally be protected."

"Don't you see, Addie?" He grabbed my arm. "You wearing that necklace is like putting a target on your back. You could be walking right into a trap."

"You know who you sound like?" I barked. "You sound just like Jimmy."

"Well maybe he was right."

"Look, you don't like my new family any more than he does. But they're my family. And this is my grandmother's necklace. I'll do her the honor of wearing it today. Out of respect for her. It's what Antoinette would have wanted."

"I can't watch you prance around like a peacock," he said.

"What is that supposed to mean?"

"It means you're in la la land, and there could be a very real criminal waiting for you with a gun." He panted as we went back and forth. "Don't make yourself a target."

"I'm not!" I gritted my teeth. "Edmond has body guards. And Louvre has security."

"You think those people will protect you?"

"Those people. Those people?" I was seething. "Who are you referring to—my family or the French?"

"No one will ever protect you like I will."

I laughed out of spite. "Oh, because you've done such a good job?"

That shut him up, so I didn't say anything. But when I brushed past him, he grabbed my arm. With every fiber of his being, he just wouldn't let go.

"Please don't wear the necklace, Addie. I'll go with you today. To the ceremony and everything. But please, just take it off. Before you get yourself killed."

I was so angry I slapped him. "If I do die today, it won't be my fault."

He stiffened and rubbed his jaw. Then he stared at me, and I wanted to cry. But Genevieve had me terrified of ruining my makeup. And the mascara wasn't waterproof.

I fled the room and ran downstairs. Adeline was on her way to the car. When I walked outside, there was a stretch limo waiting for us. Tom appeared with my mink coat and put it on for me. There was so much I wanted to say, but time was of the essence.

On the way to Louvre, Ashton had a glass of champagne. He said events like this always made him nervous, but Juliette told him he would be wonderful. Adeline sat beside them with a smile on her face. Uncle Edmond was coming in a separate car with Genevieve.

When we arrived, I was last to get out of the limousine. Tom waited with me. And I had so much to say that I couldn't manage a word. Our driver opened the door, and Tom took my hand.

"I'm sorry," I said inside the limo. "I shouldn't have slapped you. I didn't mean what I said. I—"

"Don't worry about it." He touched my cheek. "I'll jump in front of a bullet if I have to."

My eyes watered, because I didn't deserve him. He was too good for me.

"Tom." I longed to have him alone. Just the two of us. Away from all the chaos.

He leaned into the limo and kissed me. If I hadn't known it before, I knew it now. That boy really loved me. Just like Jimmy had said. Only Tom wasn't a boy. He was a man.

"Why don't we get this over with?" He pulled me into his arms and I sighed.

A red carpet led us to the museum. I hadn't expected for there to be so much press. But I guess that's the life of a royal. I clung to Tom until we were safely inside.

Genevieve had done a good job coordinating with the Louvre staff. The whole ceremony lasted about an hour. And I enjoyed every moment of it. Well, almost.

First, Edmond spoke a few words about Antoinette and the necklace. Apparently, there were some Parisian officials in the room. But I didn't know who they were until I saw Ashton shaking hands with them. I hadn't realized aristocracy was still so political.

Someone from the museum stood up to give an account of the necklace's history. Most of what she said was in French, but I detected the words Marie Antoinette in there.

Towards the end, Genevieve asked me to stand beside Edmond. In a matter of minutes, they would be taking the necklace off and placing it in a glass display case.

As I scanned the crowd of spectators, a familiar face popped up. I couldn't place him at first. I just knew he looked creepy. But then it hit me out of nowhere. Thin Man.

We'd crossed paths at the airport when I first arrived. In the gift shop, while Tom waited in line for our food. He'd been watching me then, and he was watching me now.

He reached into his jacket as I held my breath. Thankfully, he'd only been looking for a lighter for his cigarette. Then he left the room, so I wrote it off as a coincidence.

I hadn't expected the commemoration to breeze by so quickly. But the hour felt like five minutes. And even though I'd been wearing the necklace all morning, it wasn't enough.

Photographers captured every moment on camera. Especially when it was time to take the necklace off. Edmond unfastened the clasp, and the emerald slipped from my chest.

I touched my throat, feeling an immediate sense of loss. The necklace had always been heavy. But I'd felt lighter with it on. Now it felt like there was something missing.

A staff member placed the necklace on a velvet neck. Then she slid it into a glass case and shut the back panel. She used a golden key to lock it up tight, and I almost cried.

As spectators wandered off, I put my hand to the glass. The emerald necklace was trapped in a box. Like a bird in a cage. It sang to me, dying to be freed.

What had I done?

"You were wonderful," Genevieve said. "You played your part well."

She winked and left me to mingle in the museum. But I couldn't reconcile what I'd just done. Somehow, it felt like I'd been robbed. They'd taken Antoinette away from me.

Genevieve arranged a private tour for the family. Any other day, I'd have jumped at the chance to explore Louvre inside and out. But not now—when I was heartbroken.

I found a bathroom and rushed inside. Then I stood in front of the mirror and cried. I was wearing an elegant green gown and a mink fur coat. My hair was in a French twist. And I must have had on a pound of makeup. But this wasn't me. It had never felt like me.

Tom found me crying in a stall. I waited for the last woman to leave before I told him what was wrong. Maybe it was exhaustion, but I kept choking on every word.

"Do you think I did the right thing?" I asked.

"What?" He stroked my cheek. "Addie, what are you talking about?"

"With the necklace," I said. "Is that what Antoinette would have wanted?"

"I don't know. But that's what you've been saying this whole time."

He had a point. So I looked at him and nodded. Then unleashed some more tears.

"I know you love your grandmother. And I know how much her necklace meant to you." He cupped my cheeks in his hands. "But that thing has only brought danger into our lives. You did the right thing. Even Antoinette would want you to be safe."

"It feels like I'm losing her," I whimpered. "I don't want to forget her."

"You won't." He put my head on his chest. "Remember, you still have the portrait. And let's not forget everything else she left you in the attic at home. You still have her jewelry."

"I know," I sniffled. "But I've been guarding the necklace for so long."

"You don't have to anymore," he said. "Let go."

"This whole time in Paris, I've been so excited for today. Now I just feel so sad."

He dried my eyes. "I understand, but you're safe now. You can finally start living without fear.

The necklace is out of your control. No one will chase you anymore."

I nodded, because he was right. And I nuzzled his chest, because he was warm.

"I'm sorry if I'm getting makeup all over you," I said.

"It's okay. I never liked this tux anyway."

I lifted my head and laughed, feeling safe for the first time. Even at the expense of Antoinette's necklace. I hoped she would understand. I'd never intended to give up the necklace. I would have kept it forever if it hadn't been a blood emerald on my hands.

After touring Louvre, I looked out the back window of the limousine. The necklace was safe now. And I could visit anytime I liked. Antoinette's legacy would live on thanks to the museum. Today's ceremony had been a beautiful tribute to her life and lineage.

I held Tom's hand and put my head on his shoulder. He'd been right about giving up control. With the necklace gone, life was something I could finally start living.

But I feared the memory of it would haunt me forever.

Tom had been right about something else, too.

Someday, all too soon, I'd have to learn to let go.

Chapter 12

When we reached the castle, it was dark. Everyone went upstairs to change for dinner. But I slipped out the back door and walked outside. I needed a moment alone.

I treaded across the snow in my emerald gown. Then I raised my arms like a bird and spun beneath an evening flurry. It felt like I was in a snow globe.

And I didn't want anyone breaking the glass.

There was a stone bench near the woods. Two sculptures stood beside it—a little boy and a little girl. They looked like children destined to grow up and become lovers. Snow had collected on the bench. So I brushed it away and took a seat, studying the sculptures.

Tom had loved me since he was a child. Well, he'd been watching me for that long at least. I thought about how innocent that was—adoration that had nothing to do with sex.

He'd waited a lifetime to call me his. And for me, I hadn't known what I'd been missing until we met. If star crossed lovers were real, then maybe that's what we were.

I looked at the engagement ring on my finger. It was beautiful. A white diamond.

Daniel had given it to Antoinette long ago. While I didn't know the circumstances, I'm sure their proposal was romantic. It broke my heart that fate had given them such little time. If given the chance, they would have undoubtedly lived a long, happy life together.

For a split second, I wondered if history ever repeated itself.

I had a wonderful, loving man right here. And he wanted to marry me.

So what was I waiting for?

"Aren't you cold?" Tom approached, still donning his jacket and tux.

"Not really." It was only because of the mink fur coat that I hadn't frozen.

He met my eyes, and I patted the spot beside me. But there was still some snow. So I brushed enough away to make room for him and smiled when he took a seat.

I put my head on his chest and we watched the castle. The staff hung Christmas decorations today while we were gone. White lights. Wreathes. Red bows. Mistletoe.

It was simple and elegant. Just the right amount

to look classy. In my wildest dreams, I never would have imagined spending Christmas in a castle with a French count.

"Watching you today," Tom exhaled. "I couldn't believe that..."

I tugged his hand when he hesitated. "What?"

He looked into my eyes. "That you picked me."

I put my palm to his cheek, and he kissed the inside of it.

"I love you so much, Addie." He warmed my hand between his. "Did you know that?"

I nodded. "I love you, too. You have no idea how much."

"If anything ever happened to you," he lifted my chin. "I'm not like Grandpa. I'm not strong like him. I don't think I'd be able to—"

"Shh..." I covered his mouth. "Nothing is going to happen to me."

His eyes raked over my face. "I don't think you realize it. But today, you were really great up there."

"I don't know about that."

"Not one person could keep their eyes off you. You really looked like royalty."

I looked away. "It's not like I'm some princess. I was just playing a part."

"You think you're just some ordinary girl, but you're not," he said.

I blushed at his burning gaze. I wanted to be with him so much.

"You're special." He grazed my wrist. "There's something special about you, Addie. Something no one else has. I can't put my finger on it. But it drew me to you."

"That's very sweet. But there's nothing special about me."

"You're wrong." He kissed my lips tenderly. "So wrong."

"Tom, I've been doing some thinking." I put my hand on his chest. "And I wanted to apologize. I know things between us haven't been the best since we got here. I do love my family. But you're my family, too. And I want to include you in everything. I don't want to feel like I'm having to choose between you and them the rest of the time we're here."

"Addie, stop," he said. "I'm the one who should be apologizing. I know how important family is to you. When we got here, I just wanted you to be careful. I didn't want to see you get your hopes up only to have them crushed. Selfishly, I've wanted to keep you to myself. But they're good people. And they love you just as much as I do. I can see that now."

"I never meant to push you away. I—"

He interrupted me with a passionate kiss. One that took my breath away.

"I'm sorry." He pressed his forehead to mine. "Please forgive me."

"I forgive you," I chuckled. "You forgive me, too?"

"You don't need forgiving." He kissed me again. "Not like I do."

I smiled against his lips. Even in the snow, he knew how to warm my heart.

"There is something else." I caught him by surprise. "What you said before about getting married? I've thought about it. And I'm ready. It feels right."

"Are you saying...?" He was on the precipice of ecstasy.

"I want to get married here in France."

"You do?" he asked.

"Well, my family is already here. And I don't want to wait."

"But I thought you felt rushed?" He furrowed his brow.

"I did. But I don't anymore. After today, I feel at peace."

"You're sure you want to do this?" he asked.

"What—I'm finally ready and now you're getting cold feet?"

"Trust me, baby." He cupped my cheek. "My feet are very warm."

I bit my lip and squirmed. It was hard to sit still when he talked like that.

"I just want to make sure you're doing this for the right reasons," he said. "I don't want to wake up a few months from now and have you feeling like you made a mistake."

"Nothing about loving you has ever felt like a mistake."

His eyes lit up like fireworks. "You really want to do it? You want to get married?"

"Yes." I let out a breath I'd been holding. "Let's do it. I'm ready."

He shivered and took me in his arms, planting a soft kiss on my mouth. His lips were cold, but I didn't shy away. I was drawn to his warmth like a moth to the flame.

"I'll talk to your uncle and figure out the arrangements," he said.

"Thank you." I squeezed his hand. "The sooner the better."

We kissed for a little while longer, holding hands. He buried his face in my neck, and I clung to him desperately. I couldn't believe it was happening.

In one week, I had three wishes coming true.

One: I'd found my biological family, and they loved me.

Two: I was getting married to the love of my life.

Three: I was going to have one hot wedding night.

What more could a girl ask for?

Tom led me into the castle. I'd never seen him so excited. He met with Uncle Edmond privately in his office. Whatever they discussed was kept secret from me.

I headed upstairs and got ready for bed. Then I tucked myself in and looked out the window. I was in a happy little bubble. And I would murder anyone who tried to pop it.

* * *

The next three days went by in a blur. According to the law, there was a specific procedure you had to follow to get married on French soil. Neither of us were residents, so Edmond brought in a team of attorneys, notaries and advisors to speed up the process.

Tom and I called home every day. There were documents we had to have expedited across the Atlantic before the real holidays kicked in. And don't even get me started on the whole fiasco of filing for a marriage license on such short notice.

Without Edmond's help, I don't know what we would have done.

Despite everything, I kept in high spirits. I hadn't expected the wedding to be smooth sailing, especially since we were basically eloping. But we only had one major speed bump along the way. Even though it was pretty huge in relative terms.

Since I'd turned eighteen, I no longer required the permission of my legal guardians to wed. Which was excellent news, since I wasn't exactly on speaking terms with them at the moment. And Jimmy wouldn't have been able to sign in their place, no matter the relation.

Tom, on the other hand, was an entirely different story.

Since Daniel's death, he had no legal guardian. At seventeen, there was no point in throwing him back into the system. And Daniel had left his attorney with the proper documents to keep that from happening.

Once Daniel died, the court emancipated Tom as a legal subject. It's kind of like when Drew Barrymore "divorced" her parents at the age of sixteen. Tom had proof of his maturity and ability to take care of himself. Even though he was technically under age.

According to the terms of the trust, Tom could withdraw money for tuition, living expenses and upkeep on the house. Anything else was at the discretion of Walter James, Daniel's attorney. But he'd been pretty lax, and Tom never took advantage of that.

In the court's eyes, we were of legal age to wed. But our special circumstances complicated the process, which caused further delays. More paperwork. More waiting.

Usually, I would have viewed all these roadblocks as a warning sign. Maybe we were moving too fast. Maybe it wasn't right. Maybe we shouldn't have been getting married at all.

But I deflected my inhibitions, because these weren't red flags.

We were trying to pull something off that was nearly impossible. An international wedding on the cusp of Christmas. Without Edmond, it couldn't have been done.

To keep things moving along, Juliette offered to help me find a dress. Adeline tagged along, while Ashton made arrangements for Tom to have a proper tux. They hardly knew me at all, but they'd been so gracious about everything. I loved them for that.

Juliette took me to a bridal shop in Paris. The moment we walked in the door, my heart stopped. There were gowns as far as the eye could see. And since it was so close to Christmas, there was no one in the store but the women who worked there.

After taking my measurements, we talked about color and style. They showed me a notebook full of wedding dresses. Flipping through the laminated pages felt like a hassle.

It wasn't a lack of gratitude. But the stress of hasty wedding planning had gotten to me. The selection of wedding gowns left me overwhelmed. And my head already ached.

Juliette helped me narrow my choices down to twenty-five gowns. I trusted her opinion, since she'd been through this before. Plus, she knew everything about French couture.

Adeline assisted me in the dressing room. It made me think of shopping with Jeanine.

I missed her. And she would kill me when she found out. But I'd planned to talk to Tom about a small ceremony in Savannah, too. I hated not having my maid of honor here. And Tom would also be going without a best man. I suppose we could have asked Adeline and Ashton to step in. But it felt wrong when we'd already asked Jeanine and Eric to do it.

As I walked out to model another gown, Jimmy popped into my head. If I had any regrets, it was that he couldn't be here. We'd talked on the phone every day. And when Tom and I decided to get married, he was the first person I called.

Jimmy was thrilled, but my wedding would be just shy of perfect without him. I felt selfish for wanting to share this part of my life with the family I'd just met in France. But I couldn't have it both ways. Was it wrong that I wanted them all here?

In a perfect world, Jimmy could fly all night and be here for the ceremony. But I wasn't about to ask him to do that. It was so last minute and imposing, not to mention expensive. I never wanted him to feel obligated to do things for me. This was one of those times.

One of the last dresses I tried took the longest time to get on.

But it ended up being the one.

It was a lace wedding gown with a flowing white train. The top was sleeveless and corseted. But a web of sheer fabric covered the area surrounding my neck and collarbone.

When I looked in the three-way mirror, my worry ran away. It was soft and elegant—not to mention chic. Even though it was awfully sophisticated, I felt comfortable wearing it at eighteen. The dress was designed for a woman— which I was about to become.

"Oh, Addie," Juliette said.

I turned around, and they were both crying.

"You look gorgeous." And Adeline really meant it.

"I don't know." I rubbed my arms. "Won't I be cold? What about the one with long sleeves? Maybe I should get that one since it's December."

"Addie, if you don't wear that dress, I'm going to disown you."

"Mom!" Adeline looked embarrassed.

"Get the dress, Addie," Juliette said. "Trust me. It's perfect."

"Okay then," I smiled. "I will."

We spent the rest of the afternoon looking for the right veil and wedding shoes. I'd never been the best at fashion. But Juliette was turning me into a quick study.

When we returned to the castle, Tom said Edmond would like to speak to us in his office. It was already night time, and I hadn't eaten yet. But I hurried to his quarters.

"I've pulled as many strings as I can," Edmond said. "And I've finally got a date."

"Thank you so much, Uncle Edmond." I was ecstatic. "That's great."

"What day is it?" Tom asked.

"The twenty-fifth."

I hesitated, sharing a look with Tom. "But that's Christmas."

"I know." Edmond lit a cigar at his desk. "But apparently, few people get married on Christmas Day. And since the ceremony will be here, you won't have to worry about dealing with a church or local jurisdiction. They'd either be closed or unavailable anyway."

"So you're telling me the wedding has to be on Christmas Day," I said.

"By then, everything will have already been approved. It's the soonest you can wed."

I looked at Tom.

"Is the bride displeased?" Edmond asked.

"No, not at all," I insisted. "I really appreciate everything you've done for us."

"The man I've asked to officiate the ceremony is the only one available until the new year," Edmond explained. "And he is also leaving that afternoon to begin his holiday. That is the real reason why—if you're going to get married in France—it has to be then."

"I see." It wasn't how I'd planned it. But nothing ever was.

"Could we talk about it?" Tom asked. "Just me and her?"

Edmond bit the end of his cigar. "Let me know first thing in the morning."

"Thank you." I walked around his desk to give him a hug. "Truly."

I felt bad about getting married on Christmas Day. Wouldn't that ruin everyone's holiday? But the more I spoke to Juliette and Ashton, the more I realized they didn't mind. They were all so happy to have me here as part of the family. And they couldn't believe I'd chosen to share something as special as my wedding day with them.

I didn't know what to say.

It felt like I was hijacking the birth of Jesus. I didn't want to steal his thunder. Wasn't that bad luck or something? The last thing I wanted to do was be disrespectful.

But I quickly learned that we weren't the only couple to wed on December 25th. Juliette showed me wedding announcements from the past ten years. Not everyone had the picturesque June wedding you hear about in the movies. In fact, there were way more winter weddings than I'd previously thought.

So we talked about it and ultimately gave Edmond the green light. Tom and I were getting married Christmas morning in the castle. And the day was already on its way.

I'd been dancing around the idea of marriage since we got engaged. But those few days leading up to the wedding were the fastest in my life. I blinked, and they were over.

The night before the wedding, I couldn't sleep. So I made some hot cocoa in the kitchen and drank it by the Christmas tree. Even though it was my first visit, Juliette insisted I hang a few ornaments to symbolize my being a part of the family. Tom had done it, too.

I moved by the fireplace to get warm. But then something startled me.

"It's just me." Tom walked into the den. His golden eyes lit up by the fire.

I relaxed with a breath. "You scared me."

"Sorry." He leaned in and kissed my cheek. "Are you cold?"

"Freezing actually." I drank the rest of my hot cocoa.

He sat down on the hearth, patting his knee. "Come here."

I put my cup down and dove into his arms. He cradled me close, while I reveled in his body heat. If there was one constant about Tom, it was that he was always warm.

"What are you thinking about?" he asked.

"Tomorrow."

"Are you nervous?" He rubbed my back, holding me like a child.

"I'd be lying if I said I wasn't. How about you?"

"I don't know," he shrugged. "I feel pretty good about it."

"I just hope it's okay that we're getting married here on Christmas morning."

"If anyone had a problem with it, I'm sure they would have spoken up by now." He braided his fingers through mine. "They've gone through all this effort to help us get married. I'm sure they don't want it all to go to waste. Besides, I think they understand."

We'd had a quick run through of the ceremony tonight. And the officiant hadn't been able to make it. But it's not like I could get mad—it was Christmas Eve. As it turns out, we'd been fine without him because Juliette jumped in and made a fair wedding coordinator.

"I've got to find a way to pay everybody back. Especially Juliette for the dress," I said.

"Good luck with that. I already tried with your uncle and Ashton. It's almost like they feel guilty. Ashton said they've got all this money, and you were basically disinherited."

"Oh. Is that why he's spent so much money on me?" I asked.

"I guess. Not the best way to get to know your long lost cousin."

"Nope," I giggled. "Not at all."

He gazed into my eyes, and I couldn't look away.

"Thank you," I murmured. "For being here for all this."

His fingertips felt like a brushstroke over my face.

"For being with me," I breathed.

"No problem."

He pulled my hair gently, so I had to lean my head back. The pulse point in my neck was throbbing and my heart was about to explode. His eyes were on my lips.

"You know, it's a lot warmer with you in the room," I breathed.

"Is it?" He swept my hair off my neck and lowered his mouth.

"Yes," I sighed. I grabbed the back of his head to bring him closer.

He froze before our lips touched. Then he smiled.

"What is it?" I gasped.

"Maybe we should wait until the wedding."

I narrowed my eyes with a glare. "You are such a tease."

He laughed, caressing my face. "It will be worth the wait."

After he left, I gazed into the fire and played with my ring.

I was getting married tomorrow.

And I couldn't wait.

Chapter 13

If I'm being honest, I hardly slept at all. Maybe it was nerves, excitement, or a combination of the two. Either way, I tossed and turned, restless on Christmas Eve.

I lay awake and thought about the future. Deep down, I'd always hoped I would end up with Tom. I just never thought we'd be getting married so young. I was only eighteen.

But then I remembered what we had. It was rare. Like some celestial galaxy that only appeared every two hundred years. Surely, I'd be a fool to let it slip away.

I woke up early and watched the snow falling outside my window. The past few days had been a blur. And the last week had been a whirlwind. But I wasn't complaining.

It's just that life is something you can't plan. And I was learning to accept it.

Sometimes the best things come out of nowhere. They knock you off your feet. But it's the greatest gift in the world—the little blessings you don't see coming.

There was a knock on the door. And that's when it hit me. This was real.

"Come in." I sat up in bed, pooling the covers around my waist.

Juliette opened the door, and Adeline slipped in behind her. My wedding dress was hanging up in the closet. And I couldn't believe—in just a few hours—I'd be walking down the aisle in it.

"I brought you breakfast." Adeline put a silver platter on my bed.

"Thank you," I said. "That's so sweet."

There were biscuits and jelly, scrambled eggs and cured ham. I wanted to stuff my face after what had happened the morning of the commemoration. I'd left the house starving.

But Juliette told me to relax and take my time. So I nursed a cup of hot tea and filled my plate. There was more than enough food to go around. And I didn't want to see any going to waste. But Juliette and Adeline had already eaten, so I told them to save the rest for later.

"Can you believe it?" Adeline asked. "You're getting married."

"I know." I picked the bedding beneath me. "Is it weird?"

"What?" Adeline furrowed her brow.

"Just that I'm getting married so young. Won't

everyone think I'm pregnant?"

"Don't worry about what everyone else thinks," Juliette advised. "I never do."

I went to the bathroom and brushed my teeth. While I would have preferred a better night's sleep, my reflection didn't look terrible. Thanks to the miracle of cosmetics, I'd have plenty of help when it came to giving me a fresh-faced look.

"This is a wedding." Juliette set a trunk down on the counter. "So I brought the works."

I took a seat in front of the mirror. She opened every compartment and showed me the options available. Foundation, concealer, powder, blush, eye shadow, lipstick, nail polish in every palette you can imagine—you name it, she had it.

"I'm not so good at this," I said.

"Why don't you just show me what you like? And we'll work from there."

"Okay." I gave Juliette a smile. I know she was technically my cousin-in-law, since she was Ashton's wife. We weren't blood related. But she was the closest thing to a real life aunt I'd ever had. And I'd really missed having women in the family who I could talk to.

I washed my face and then patted it dry. Since it was winter, my tan had mostly faded away. But Juliette had a bottle of tinted moisturizer that was like water for your skin. Being in the dry cold, I longed for hydration. So it was the perfect foundation.

Adeline brushed my hair while her mother

showed me palettes for my eyes. We settled on smoky gray with a hint of forest green. Juliette used a special technique, blending one color along the crease in my eyelid. She then shaped the brow bone with a lighter shade.

Mascara was the final touch where eye makeup was concerned, and it was a miracle worker. My lashes lengthened without any clumping, and the volume was incredible. It was a bold, black hue that made my eyes pop.

"It's waterproof." Juliette smiled in the mirror. "Just in case."

"Thank you." If I did cry, they would be tears of joy.

Juliette shaped my brows and then smoothed out the concealer beneath my eyes. I sucked in my cheeks so she could apply a conservative swoop of blush. Then she blended my neck and jawline, making sure the foundation wasn't uneven or splotchy.

Lipstick was the only cosmetic left. I'd chosen a shade of rose. Not quite red, so to speak. It was more of a dark pink with lots of pigmentation. Like raspberries.

"Thank you for helping me with all of this." I pressed my lips together.

"Of course." Juliette touched my shoulder. "Now, what to do with your hair?"

"Well, I don't want it all up. But I don't want it in my face either," I said.

"I know just the trick." She pulled my hair

behind my back and went to work.

As she styled my hair, I talked to Adeline about life in Savannah. She had never left Europe before so she was very curious about America. I hoped they would come visit us when we returned to the states. We had plenty of room, and I would miss them.

Just thinking about it made me sad. So I pushed the thought of parting with my new relatives to the back of my mind. And I focused on my wedding day instead.

"What do you think?" Juliette gave me a mirror to see the complete do.

She'd put the top of my hair in an elegant braid. The rest of my locks hung in loose waves. Since I'd chosen to wear a veil, it was perfect. I couldn't have asked for more.

"I love it!" I handed her the mirror. "It's like you read my mind."

Juliette grinned ear to ear. "Now, time for the best part. The dress!"

Adeline squealed in excitement and ran in the bedroom to get it. When she came back, I stripped off my pajamas and shivered until the dress was on. Juliette helped lace the corset, while I wondered if Tom would have a hard time getting it off tonight.

While I was putting my shoes on, someone knocked on the door. Juliette offered to answer it, while Adeline fastened the straps on my heels. They were only a few inches off the ground, giving me just the right amount of height since Tom was so tall.

I heard Edmond's voice in the bedroom. "I wanted to see the bride before her big day." He peeked into the doorway and saw me standing by the mirror. "Addison."

I lit up at the sight of him. It felt so good to be surrounded by family.

"My dear." He took my hand. "You look stunning."

"Thank you, Uncle Edmond." I kissed his cheek. "You've been so good to me."

"It's been a long time coming. I know you've made my sister proud."

I felt the threat of tears, but Juliette warned me about ruining my makeup.

"There's no need for tears," he said. "I just wanted to deliver a gift from the groom."

My heart warmed. I'd never been expecting a gift. Tom was so thoughtful.

Jimmy walked into the room, and I held my breath.

"You didn't think I'd miss my little girl's big day now, did you?" he quipped.

I dove into his arms and held him tight. He patted my back while I cried. Instead of scolding me, this time, Juliette stepped out with the others to give us some privacy.

"What are you doing here?" I dried my eyes.

"Tom wanted to surprise you. He knew how much it would mean to you if I came."

"I love him, Dad." The name felt so natural on my tongue. "I really do."

"I know you do, kid." He rubbed my shoulder. "Don't be afraid of it."

"I'm not afraid." I bowed my head, feeling the exhaustion set in. "I just—"

"Just always remember how special it is between the two of you."

I nodded and buried my face in his chest. "I can't believe you're here."

"Well, believe it. Your uncle has even offered to put me up in this castle." He looked at the marble in the bathroom. "I can't believe this place. No wonder you left me at home."

"Hey!" I giggled, playfully slapping his arm.

He laughed and took my hand. "Why don't you sit down?"

I pulled out the chair facing the mirror and eased into it. Now that I was ready for the ceremony, I had to be especially careful in the dress. I didn't want to tear it.

"I wanted to give you something," he said.

"You don't have to give me anything. Just you being here is—"

"Listen, Addie, I want to. So let me."

"Okay," I nodded, sitting up straight in the chair.

Jimmy pulled a string of pearls out of his pocket. "These belonged to my mother."

I looked at him in the mirror. I didn't know what to say.

"After your mother disappeared, I never thought I'd have anyone to give them to." He slid the pearls around my neck and fastened the clasp. "Now you have something from my family, too."

I touched the pearls. "They're beautiful."

"Just like you." He kissed my forehead.

"Thank you." I tried not to tear up. "For everything."

Juliette came in the room with my veil. "It's time."

I stood so she could clip the veil to my hair. "I feel nervous."

"You'll be fine," Jimmy said. "I'm sure he's nervous, too."

Juliette lowered the veil over my face. "Are you ready?"

I answered her with a nod, and Adeline couldn't contain her excitement. Juliette handed me a bouquet of white roses. There were a few pieces of holly in the mix.

"Since it's Christmas," Adeline explained.

I admired the flowers. "Thank you. They're perfect."

Adeline beamed as her mother cleared the way. Jimmy stuck his arm out, and I looped mine through it. Then we walked into the hallway and headed for the staircase.

"Promise me you'll still stop by and see your old man," Jimmy whispered.

"Dad, I'm getting married. It doesn't change anything between us."

"I know, but you'll have your own life now with your husband."

"Nothing is ever going to take me away from you," I said. "I promise."

He smiled, and it reminded me of the first time we met. If you'd told me six months ago that I was going to find my true father and marry my true love, I'd say you were nuts. I guess that's why they don't make crystal balls that let you see what's going to happen next.

It would ruin the suspense.

When I heard the wedding march, the last tinge of reality set in. There were rose petals on the stairs. So I held on to Jimmy's arm to make sure I didn't slip.

My heart felt like it might beat out of my chest. Nothing in life had prepared me for this. But fear had nothing to do with my nerves. I just wanted to make sure I did this right.

We were only a few hundred yards away from the parlor, but I wasn't ready to look up. I dug my fingernails into Jimmy's arm and took a breath. Then I bit the bullet and jumped.

Tom stood at the end of the aisle in a black tuxedo. There was a white rose pinned to his breast pocket. He looked devastatingly handsome, and I couldn't believe he was mine.

By what stretch of the imagination would this beautiful man choose me?

When he saw me, it was like the world stopped spinning on its axis. Our eyes met in a burning gaze—one that could have scorched a thousand suns. And I felt the flames.

I don't remember walking towards him.

It was almost like I floated there. And when we met, Tom put his hand in mine.

We turned toward each other, as the officiant began the ceremony.

My ears were buzzing with the beat of my heart.

So I didn't hear a word he said.

All I know is—my future was where Tom belonged. Because I couldn't imagine a day in my life without him. It simply wouldn't do. I had to be wherever he was, right alongside him. It was the only thing that made sense. The only reason why we'd been through hell.

Love trumps everything. And now that we were joined as one, there was nothing that could keep us apart. I knew in my heart that we'd survived the worst.

The war was over. All that was left to do was live.

I do.

Tom said those words, and I felt it in my soul. The butterflies I'd harvested were gone. Sappy, mushy feelings of love and lust had replaced them.

"I do," I echoed.

"I believe you each have something prepared." The officiant left a finger in his notebook and closed it.

"Yes," Tom breathed. He reached into his

jacket pocket and grabbed a piece of folded paper. "All right if I go first?"

"Yes." The officiant shot him an encouraging smile.

My vows were personal, so I knew his would be, too. We'd been through so much together that words couldn't quite explain. But we would try.

"Addie, I saw you for the first time when I was eight years old. You were the prettiest girl I'd ever seen. I couldn't stop thinking about you then, and I have no plans to start now."

I saw his hand shake and wondered if I still made him nervous. He'd told me I did once, and I'd never forgotten it.

"I promise to give you a long life of comfort and happiness. I promise to love, honor, and protect you no matter the cost. I'll always be there as your shoulder to cry on. I'll never deny you anything. And I'll never leave your side—no matter what the future holds. I'll love you 'til the day I die. And I'll do whatever you want..."

Tears flooded his eyes, and I melted on the inside.

"...whatever you ask, whatever makes you happy. Because I can't believe I'm getting to spend the rest of my life with a girl—I mean, woman, like you."

I blushed as a tear trickled down my cheek.

"Is it my turn?" I looked at Adeline, and she handed me a journal. I'd used it to write my wedding vows since we'd been in Paris.

I felt his eyes on me as I flipped to the first page. It felt like an out-of-body experience, because I'd yet to get used to the fact that it was our wedding day.

"Tom, I never knew what love was until you showed me. I've never thought of you as a boy or a guy. Because you're not. You're a man."

He smoldered, as I caught him brooding.

"At our age, I know how rare that is. And I know how lucky I am. When I'm with you, I'm the person I want to be. I love you so much it scares me. But I promise to keep loving you with everything I have in me. Until the breath leaves my body, I'm yours. And I promise to spend the rest of my life being the woman you deserve. Because you are the best man I've ever known."

Tom smiled, but there were tears involved. I wanted to be in his arms. But even more than that, I wanted to kiss him.

He grabbed my hands, and we stayed like that for the remaining formalities. I believe I would have repeated anything the officiant said. So long as I ended up in Tom's arms.

For the longest time, I never thought he'd say it. But then the words were out there. And I couldn't believe it.

"You may kiss the bride."

Tom lifted the veil over my face and crushed his lips to mine. I clung to the lapels on his jacket and melted into him. We were drowning in tears by the time we came up for air.

As we walked back down the aisle, I noticed Ashton and Edmond for the first time. They'd been there all along—in my peripheral vision—but I'd been preoccupied. Juliette and Adeline were all smiles. I thanked them both, because I couldn't have done it without them.

My eyes landed on Jimmy last. He kissed my cheek and shook Tom's hand. Words could not express how much it meant to me that he'd flown here for the wedding.

I had Tom to thank for that.

After the ceremony, we had a small reception in the ballroom, where Tom and I shared our first dance. There was a seven course meal and the most elaborate cake I'd ever seen. I told Edmond we would find a way to pay him back for all of this.

He simply smiled and said, "Merry Christmas."

All in all, it was the best day of my life. I'd never been happier.

My long lost uncle had invited me to his castle. My long lost cousin had showered me with enough presents for a decade of Christmases. And my long lost father had walked me down the aisle on my wedding day. So I could marry my one and only true love, Tom.

I had so much to be grateful for. Despite the past, life was amazing.

And I had every intention to start living it. With my new husband.

When it was time to leave, my family lined the

drive to see us off. I gave everyone a hug individually and thanked them a million times for everything. They had been too kind.

"Make sure you take good care of my girl," Jimmy said as he shook Tom's hand.

"I will, sir." Tom patted him on the back.

"Thank you for coming." I kissed Jimmy on the cheek. "It really meant a lot."

He hugged me close. "I wouldn't miss it for the world."

"So you're staying in the castle tonight?" I asked.

"Yeah." He looked at the estate behind him. "Can you imagine that?"

"Edmond is a good man," I said. "Just like my husband." Tom beamed as I looped my arm through his. "And my father."

Jimmy pulled me into his arms. "I love you, kid."

"I love you, too, Dad."

We broke apart so I could leave with Tom. Edmond had a stretch limo waiting for us in the drive. He'd also reserved the honeymoon suite at a hotel in downtown Paris.

If I lived a hundred years, I didn't know how I'd be able to thank him for his kindness. Uncle Edmond had been exceptionally gracious to me—a long lost relative. And I had no idea what I'd done to deserve it.

I got in the limousine with Tom and waved at my loving new family. A few tears ran down my cheek as we drove away. Their image became a blurred memory, but I tried to suck it up.

Everyone cries at weddings.

"You all right?" Tom touched my cheek.

We were still in formal attire—his tux and my gown. While we could have changed at the castle, it was better not to. I wanted him to unwrap me like a Christmas present.

"Yeah." I kissed him on the mouth as his hand slid around my waist. "Never better."

Chapter 14

On the way to the hotel, we kissed in the backseat. There was a partition blocking the driver from view. And I was thankful for the privacy. I couldn't keep my hands off of Tom.

Edmond had good taste. Because the hotel he'd chosen for our wedding night was absolutely beautiful—all lit up for the holidays. There was a Christmas tree in the lobby.

"I keep forgetting what day it is," I said.

Tom squeezed my hand as we moved to the check-in desk. Our room was under the name Sutton. And it was the first time I thought about the fact that I was Addie Sutton now.

Addie Smith was no more—it was a surname I was happy to get rid of.

But Sutton? Well, that was the name I should have had all along. It tied me to Daniel. As if it weren't enough being bound to Tom. Maybe it was only the last name, but it felt like I was adopting a new identity.

It was a clean slate, a fresh start.

The perfect way to start my life with him.

"Ready?" He had the room key in his hand. It was gold plated and engraved with the number of our room—1959.

"Yes," I smiled.

He took my hand and we rode the elevator to the nineteenth floor. I'm sure we looked odd not having any bags. But we were only staying the night. In the morning, we'd return to the castle, pack up and embark on our honeymoon.

Tom had kept the destination a secret, so I didn't know where. It was driving me crazy. But it also made me gush over his sweetness. He'd put so much effort into spoiling me.

"Where are you taking me?" I whined.

"It's a surprise." He pulled me into his arms. "But I promise you'll love it."

The elevator dinged, and the doors opened on the nineteenth floor. We strolled down the hall arm in arm. Our room was at the end of the corridor. For a second there, I'd almost forgotten we had the honeymoon suite.

Tom unlocked the door and swept me off my feet. I let out a little yelp and curled my arms around his neck. We crossed the threshold and the door clicked shut behind us.

"Wow." My jaw dropped as he set me down. "This place is beautiful. Look at the view."

You could see the Eiffel Tower from our bedroom window. Fireworks went off in the night—a preview of the New Year's Eve to come. I couldn't believe a new year was already on its way. But I had a feeling it was going to be the best one yet.

"It's breathtaking," I said.

"So are you." He was standing behind me, his breath on my neck. He helped me take my coat off and hung it up by the door. "Do you want to see the rest of the room?"

We'd only been in the bedroom so far.

"No." I looked him in the eye. "Not now."

He caught my drift and took his jacket off. His eyes were on me as he turned the radio on. They were playing "Have Yourself a Merry Little Christmas." And while it may have been in French, I'd recognize that tune in any language.

Tom held out his hand. "May I have this dance?"

I slid my hand into his as we established a rhythm. We danced slowly, soaking up the warmth and love we shared. But when the song ended, he turned the music off.

"What is this?" I found a bottle of champagne in an ice bucket.

Tom came to my side and read the card attached. "Love, Uncle Edmond."

"That's so sweet but—"

"Do you want some?" Tom put two glasses on the table. "You know, the legal drinking age here is sixteen. It's not like he did anything wrong."

"Oh," I blinked. "I forgot about that."

Tom opened the bottle and poured each of us a glass. "You know, I really think I'm starting to like Europe. It's growing on me."

"Those are words I never thought I'd hear you say," I teased. Then I went to take a sip of champagne.

"Wait," he stopped me. "We have to make a toast."

"Oh, what should we toast to?" I asked.

Tom raised his glass. "To a long and happy life together."

We clinked glasses, and I had my first taste of champagne. It was sweeter than I'd imagined. But it was sour, too. I couldn't tell if I liked it or not.

"Oh, look." Tom picked up a box of chocolates. "From Ashton, Juliette and Adeline. Do you want one?"

I closed all the blinds. "Not now."

"Okay." Tom put the chocolates down, along with his champagne.

"I was wondering if you could help me out of my dress," I said.

He cleared his throat. "Umm, yeah. I think I can manage that."

I took my shoes off first and then unclipped the veil. He walked up behind me and swept the hair off my neck. When he left a kiss there, I closed my eyes.

"It's a corset," I rasped.

"Yeah, I've got it." He pulled at the ribbon, slowly but surely unlacing the gown. "Sorry it's taking me so long."

"No, it's fine." I didn't want him feeling rushed.

When he got the hang of it, I stared at the wedding band on my finger. I thought about the ring and everything it represented—a new addition to my hand. Surely, our love was meant to last a lifetime.

"All done," he said, slightly out of breath.

I turned around and felt the straps loosen over my shoulders. "Keep going."

He swallowed and pushed the straps down my arms. I held on to him as the fabric slid over my hips. Then it lay in a pool of white at my feet.

"Do you mind if I undress you?" I asked.

"No." He moistened his mouth. "Go ahead."

He'd already taken his bow tie off, so I took the liberty of unbuttoning his shirt. When I reached the last button, he was staring at me. I ran my fingers over his stomach, tracing every dip and shallow.

He shut his eyes as I kissed his chest, putting my lips where his heart was. I'd never seen a naked man before, but I wasn't afraid. Sex was normal, natural. And not only did I love this man, he was my husband.

I pulled a sheer slip over my head, and his eyes glazed over my body. I was wearing a white lacy set of lingerie that Juliette helped me pick out at the bridal shop. It was classy and elegant, but still very sexy. At least I thought so.

When I felt brave enough, I looked into his eyes and begged, "Make love to me."

He claimed my mouth in an instant, threading his fingers in my hair. I rocked forward and wrapped my arms around him, returning every kiss. Pretty soon, we were going to spontaneously combust.

"Take off your clothes," I said. "Please."

So he stepped out of his shoes and shucked his socks and pants. I pushed his shirtsleeves down his arms, and his button down fell to the floor. Then there was nothing but undergarments keeping us apart.

Tom pressed his hand into my back, as I clung to his masculine frame.

So tall. So strong. So warm.

He picked me up in his arms, and we lay down on the mattress. Because it was so cold, we slipped under the covers. Then there was nothing but skin between us.

"Tom?" I ran my hand over his naked back. "Turn out the light."

He did what I asked him to, giving me his undivided attention. Sex was something we'd wrestled with over the past few months. But I hardly felt like dodging the subject tonight.

Tonight was the night.

I'm not going to lie—the first time wasn't as good as I'd expected. We were a mess. Sloppy.

Impatient. Inexperienced.

But as the night wore on, things changed.

I learned the contours of his body as he explored mine. We'd been lost without a road map, but we were finding our way. Especially when he made me feel things I'd never known were humanly possible.

I wrapped my body around him and scratched his back. He held my hands and buried his face in my neck. His stubble left my skin feeling incredibly sensitive, and oh so good.

In the darkness, all I cared about was his body and mine. He'd branded my soul in more ways than one. And I knew that I wouldn't be able to live without this heavenly touch day and night.

Tom lay down beside me and cupped my cheek in his hand. "Baby. Why are you crying?"

I took a staggering breath. "I love you so much."

He traced the curves of my waist and then tucked a lock of hair behind my ear. "I love you, too."

I put my head on his chest and touched his ribs. Then I closed my eyes and kissed his salty skin. We were covered in sweat, but I'd never felt so at peace.

"Thank you." He stroked my arm.

"For what?" I asked.

"For sharing this with me." He braided his fingers through mine, and I peered up at him. "We have a part of each other that no one else will ever have. No matter what happens, we'll always have that."

"You know, you were right." My fingers walked the length of his collarbone. "I'm glad we waited until tonight."

"Why?" He petted my hair.

"Because it was worth the wait."

He touched the string of pearls around my neck. "Where did you get these?"

"Jimmy gave them to me," I said. "They were his mother's."

He grinned and toyed with my engagement ring. "Now you have something from both of your grandmothers."

Nuzzling his chest, I took a breath and closed my eyes. "We need to have a talk."

"Okay." He rubbed my bare back. "About what?"

I leaned my head back and looked at him. "Do you really want five children?"

"Yeah." He tucked a loose lock behind my ear. "Why not?"

"You do realize that I'm the one who has to shoot them out, right?"

He laughed. "I don't know if it's like loading a shotgun, honey."

"But what if it's exactly like loading a shotgun?" I giggled.

On a serious note, Tom lifted my chin. "Don't you want kids?"

"Of course I do. Maybe a boy and a girl. Or

two."

He lovingly caressed my face, focused on my pleasure.

"It's really important for me to have kids of my own."

"Biological," he said. "So your crazy temper will become a hereditary trait."

"I do not have a crazy temper!"

He pointed at me, lightly grazing the tip of my nose.

"What about you? You get angry too sometimes, Mr. Sutton."

"I know." He hovered above me. "That's because you're infuriating."

He covered me in sumptuous kisses, planting his lips all over my body. I put my head on his shoulder and held him close, as we clung together in the night.

We stayed up for hours, learning how to make love. From the first taste, I'd been addicted. And I didn't see how we'd ever get enough of each other. Only time would tell.

For now, I was swimming in a bubble of happiness. I'd never felt so free in my life. Like I was actually living for the first time—the way mother nature had intended.

We dozed off when it felt like we'd participated in a decathlon. I put my head on his chest and rested my hand on his stomach. My leg was curled around his hips as I dreamed.

But then the phone rang at the crack of dawn.

We'd—quite literally—just gone to sleep. I grumbled and moaned, but Tom wouldn't answer it. He was worn out, practically unconscious. So I leaned over him and answered the hotel phone.

"What?" I didn't even cheer up when I realized it was only Edmond.

"Addie, are you sitting down?" he asked.

"Yes. Why?"

"Someone broke into the Louvre last night and stole the necklace."

Chapter 15

A car arrived for us at the hotel. Edmond sounded terrified, and it had me worried sick. Surely, he wouldn't delay my honeymoon except in the case of extreme circumstances.

Check-out was a breeze, because we had no clothes to pack. Last night, my thoughts started and ended with Tom. Even now, I couldn't stop thinking about the way he'd touched me.

To be honest, I couldn't wait for him to do it again. But our marriage bed would simply have to wait. I couldn't fly away to some unforeseen location if my family could be in danger. And when it came to the necklace, danger never seemed to be very far.

On the way to the castle, I couldn't sit still. I kept rubbing my palms together and cracking my knuckles. To a stranger, we must have looked ridiculous—with Tom in his tuxedo and me donning my wedding gown from the night before.

But in all fairness, I hadn't planned on being roused from bed so close to sunrise. Especially the morning after my wedding night.

"I'm sure everything is fine." Tom took my hand.

"Then why did Edmond sound like he was about to have a heart attack?" I asked.

He released my hand and looked out the window. Apparently, the cynics were right. The first year of marriage is the hardest. And I didn't even have a full twenty-four hours under my belt yet.

The castle gates came into view, and I moved to the edge of my seat. As soon as we reached the entrance, I opened my own door and hurried up the front steps. I found my whole family in the den watching a local news report. They flashed to footage of Louvre.

I couldn't understand a word, since the newscaster was speaking in French. But the video taken from the security camera required no translation. On Christmas night, a thief broke into Louvre and smashed the glass case surrounding the necklace.

"How is that possible?" I scoffed. "I thought Louvre had alarms and guards and—"

"He disabled them," Ashton said. "It's not like he doesn't have the experience."

"Who?" I stared at the screen.

"Valjean." Edmond got out of his chair and

walked towards me. "He's a jewel thief. And he's been robbing mansions all over Paris since last summer."

"You know him?" I felt Tom behind me.

"I know of him." He took a cigar out of his pocket and left the room.

"He's been in the news since May," Ashton said. "He's the best."

"But how do you even know it's him?" I pointed at the TV. "He's wearing a mask."

"It's him, dear cousin." Ashton patted my shoulder. "Trust me. I know."

"Well, what do you want me to do about it?" I asked.

Ashton looped his arm through mine. "Come with me."

I turned back to look at Tom, and he followed my footsteps.

"No." Ashton stopped. "Without your husband."

While I disliked the arrangement, I agreed to it. The sooner I met with Edmond, the sooner we could be on our honeymoon. I couldn't wait to be miles away from here.

Ashton led me into his father's office and closed the door behind us.

"Sit down, Addison." Edmond had never been so stern with me. "Now."

I swallowed and took a seat, girding my loins. "Uncle Edmond, I—"

"Do not speak, child. Not until you are spoken

to."

My cheeks flushed in embarrassment as I relaxed in my chair. I hadn't been scolded like that in such a long time. His bitter tone stung, and I felt like crying.

"The necklace is missing," Edmond said. "And I want you to find it."

"Me? I'm just some American girl in Europe for the holidays. I don't know anything about catching a jewel thief. I just got married for God's sake."

"Look at her, Ashton. Married one day and already acting all high and mighty."

I bit my lip. "I didn't mean to be disrespectful. But I'm not your girl."

"You are the only one who can find the necklace, Addie. And you'll stay in this castle until you've done so. Is that understood?" He blew out a puff of smoke.

I turned to Ashton for allegiance, but he wasn't saying anything. My mind raced with curious thoughts. All this time, they'd been so warm and generous to me. But the truth of the matter is I didn't know them at all. By now, they were just a pack of familiar strangers.

"I'm leaving today on my honeymoon," I said.

"That will have to wait." Edmond eyed me from his elegant hand-carved desk. I'd hate to know who must have suffered chopping that wood. Someone else had broken his back, all so Edmond could sit there and gawk on his throne of power and deception.

"You can't keep me here held hostage," I demanded. "I'm leaving."

When I moved towards the door, Ashton blocked me. "I'm sorry."

I glared at Edmond over my shoulder. "You can't do this. I won't let you!"

I charged towards him, but Ashton pinned my arms behind my back. He made sure I held still while Edmond rose from his desk, making his way towards me.

"Now, I won't have you mentioning any of this to that new husband of yours." Edmond waited for my acquiescence. "All that was said remains in this room. Correct?"

I nodded when I saw no other option.

"Let her go, son," Edmond barked. "Don't be so dramatic." He left the room, and I didn't know how to feel. The betrayal seeped into my bones like tree roots in a swamp.

"You know, there was a time when I wanted to be an actor." Ashton gave me a sheepish grin.

I gritted my teeth and slapped him. "Don't ever do that again."

"I'm sorry. I was just—"

"I thought you were my family," I accused. "I trusted you."

"Don't be so quick to judge, Addie. You don't know what the loss of that necklace means to him." Ashton took a seat in the chair I'd left abandoned.

"What do you mean?" I furrowed my brow.

"I'm talking about your grandmother. Her death has haunted him for years. And it's the way she died, too. Drowning herself in the river like Ophelia."

"Antoinette didn't kill herself," I exclaimed. "She was murdered!"

"Well, that's what you think. Papa was told a different story." He stood up and brushed past me, opening the door. I caught a whiff of his cologne that was so familiar to me now.

"Was any of it real?" I asked. "Or were you just pretending to love me?"

"We do love you, Addie. All of us. You just can't see it right now. If you did, you wouldn't be questioning a thing we've said. You'd know we're only trying to protect you."

"I don't believe you." I walked out the door. "I wish I'd never come to Paris."

I ran down the corridor and bumped into Adeline.

"Sorry," she muttered. "Are you all right?"

I wanted to tell her everything—my new friend. But her grandfather had sworn me to secrecy. For whatever reason, I wouldn't even be able to tell Tom—my new husband.

When he appeared, I backed away from him and cried all the way to my room. He chased me down the hall and put his hand in the door when I tried to shut it in his face. Overpowered by his masculinity, I took a few steps back and collapsed on the bed.

Burying my face in the sheets, I cried for a variety of reasons.

(1) I was trapped in a castle by my very own uncle.

(2) Acquiring the necklace was my only way out.

(3) I might never be able to go on my honeymoon.

I heard the door close, but my tears were like a dam that had finally broken loose. There was no hope of drying it up anytime soon. My tears were a flood of panic.

"Hey." Tom touched my back and sat down beside me. "Addie."

But I kept right on crying. Because there was nothing else to do at this point.

"Baby." He tried to lull me near, but I wouldn't budge. So he lay across the mattress and pulled me into his arms. I buried my face in his chest and held on to him.

"Tom." I choked on my words. I lifted my eyes to look at him, and he wiped my tears with a smile. "I'm sorry," I whimpered. "I'm so, so sorry."

"About what?" Half of his smile dipped into a frown.

"We have to stay here until they figure out where the necklace is."

"What?" He cradled my body. "We're supposed to be on a flight to Italy."

I lit up like a firework. "Is that where you were taking me?"

"Yeah," he deflated in disappointment. "Rome. Naples. Florence."

"Sounds amazing," I sighed. "I'll bet it would have been a beautiful honeymoon."

"Why do you have to say it like that?" he asked. "Like it's in the past tense."

"Because it is." I traced the edge of his jawline. "Someone stole my grandmother's necklace. According to Edmond, we're not safe until it's been recovered."

"Really?" he said. "How does he know that?"

I felt bad for lying to Tom. I'd always longed for total honesty in our relationship. Precarious circumstances had hindered that in the past. Marriage could have been a fresh start to no longer keeping secrets between us. I guess that would never happen now.

"He just does. But I trust him. Don't you?" I gazed into his eyes, wishing he could read between the lines. In that moment, I wished I had a better way of getting him the message.

"Yeah. Of course." He kissed my hair and wrapped his arms around me. "We can go to Italy another time. After everything that's happened, your safety is most important."

With my head on his chest, it took all I could to keep him from hearing me cry.

"You're probably just tired," he said. "It's been a busy couple of days."

Tom pulled the covers back and tucked me in. Then he lay down in bed beside me. I'd hardly slept the past two nights. The first from nervous excitement. The second from sex. That was the only reason why I drifted off in his arms so easily.

When I woke up, they might be expecting me at the guillotine.

* * *

I must have slept for hours, because I didn't even bother to get undressed. I'd yet to recover from the night before, so I was still sore and stiff. Regardless, I felt like someone was watching me. It was the burn of a steady gaze that made blush rise to my cheeks.

"Hey." I saw Tom sitting in a chair by my bed. "How long have you been doing that?"

"What?" His eyes were golden brown like whiskey. He never blinked.

"Just sitting there, watching me."

"A couple of hours."

I pushed myself up and leaned against the headboard. "What's wrong?"

He took my hand in his. "Why do I get the feeling that there's something you're not telling me?"

I averted my gaze, but his amber irises were like an arrow sent straight for my heart.

"I'm not allowed to talk about it."

He stared me down. "Here at the castle? Or at all?"

"At all, I guess."

"No." He stood up and tossed me my mink fur coat. "Let's go for a walk."

I put my shoes on and followed him into the courtyard. A blanket of snow covered the ground. I thought about my winter wonderland. A pretty snow globe.

Only now, an outsider had shattered the glass.

"Why won't you tell me what's going on?" Tom stuck his hands in his pockets.

My arm was looped through his as I leaned on him. "What do you want me to say?"

"The truth." He stopped in his tracks. "You're my wife now, Addison."

I kept walking until something strange caught my eye. "It can't be."

We stumbled upon a bed of roses. Some red, some white.

"How can they be blooming now? In the middle of winter? It's snowing." I bent over and picked a white rose. "This must be the place Edmond told me about. The day we arrived, he told me Antoinette spent a lot of time in a rose garden."

"Well, I guess this is it."

I clutched the rose in my hand to feel closer to her. But in the end, I held it too tight.

A thorn pricked my finger, and I dropped the rose. Tom attended to my hand, while I looked at the ground. Fallen rose petals lay in the snow. They were covered in blood.

"Edmond is holding me hostage in the castle.

He wants the necklace, and he won't let me leave until I've found it. For some reason, he believes I'm the only one who can."

Tom ripped his shirt and wrapped my finger with a piece of it.

"Aren't you going to say something?" I asked.

"Not now," he said. "You don't know who could be watching us."

"You believe me?" I'd thought Edmond might have him fooled.

"Yes." He caressed my cheek, and I softened at his touch. "Every word."

"What should I do?" I gasped. "Tom, tell me what to do."

"Come with me." He took my hand. "We'll think of something."

* * *

A few hours later, Tom requested that the two of us have dinner in our room. Edmond didn't object—to my surprise. In fact, he even sent up a four course meal.

We dined on soup, salad, creamy chicken pasta and breadsticks. I hadn't eaten a thing all day. So I was especially grateful when he sent up a pint of mandarin sorbet. I'd never tasted the flavor before, but it was delicious. It might have even been an apology.

"You look tired," Tom said.

"Well, there's one way to fire up your new bride."

"Come here." He pulled me into his lap and

ran his hands down my waistline.

"I guess we could still have a decent honeymoon right here." I braided my hands at the nape of his neck, holding his gaze. "I mean, we are in a castle."

"Right you are, Mrs. Sutton. That's why I've already started running a hot bath."

"Oh." I leaned in but paused before we kissed. "Is that so?"

"Yes." He molded his mouth to mine. "Let's get you undressed."

I soaked up the light shining from his eyes. "I have a surprise."

The corner of his mouth twitched as I slid from his lap and escaped into the bathroom. He came after me and shut the door behind us. Then he locked it as well.

Turning towards him, I unfastened the sash on my silk robe and let it fall to the floor. He hadn't known at the time. But I wasn't wearing anything underneath it.

Pleased by the look on his face, I sank into the warm water and rested my head against the tub. He popped the cork on a bottle of red wine and then handed me a glass.

"Aren't you going to join me?" I purred.

Tom knelt down on the tile and devoured me with kisses. When we came up for air, he filled my glass with red wine. Then we said "cheers" and he drank straight out of the bottle.

I watched him take his shirt off and set my

wine glass aside. Then I pulled him closer and kissed him until he had fully undressed. He climbed into the tub, and water lapped over the edges. And when he reached for me, I squealed.

He left kisses down my neck and back. I ran my fingers through his hair, putting my body all over him. In one night, he took me to every place known to woman.

I curled my arms around his body and squeezed him tight. It was an intimate embrace. The best hug I'd ever given. Or received. It was the kind of love to last a lifetime.

We ended up in bed with the covers tangled all around us. I looked into his eyes and touched his beautiful face. "My husband," I whispered in the dark.

"My wife." He kissed the cut on my finger left by a thorn.

"I love you, Thomas Sutton."

He cupped my cheek as I leaned into his palm. "Not like I love you, Addison Sutton."

I wrapped my arms around him and he rose above me, pressing my body into the mattress. We made love slowly in the night. I'd savor the memory for years to come.

* * *

I woke hours later to the sound of Tom breathing beside me. I suppose he was too young to snore, but it was the next best thing. For ten minutes, I sat up on my elbow and watched him. It felt like I was in heaven, just teetering on the edge of paradise.

But then I heard a noise in the hall. And I didn't have the heart to wake Tom.

My beautiful husband was sleeping so peacefully. It looked like he was smiling.

So I slipped into a night gown and pulled my robe on over it. Then I went into the hall and closed the door behind me, careful not to disturb Tom. There was a lit candle waiting for me outside the door. Without it, I wouldn't have been able to see anything.

With the candle as my guide, I weaved my way through the castle. A mouse darted out in the hall, and I almost screamed. But the noise I'd heard earlier had been discovered, so I took a breath in the hope of relaxing. Until I saw what the rodent was following.

There was a trail of blood in the corridor. And it looked fresh.

Curiosity got the best of me, and I kept walking. The trail led me to the portrait room. The one Adeline had shown me when we first arrived at the castle.

I put one foot in front of the other until I reached her. I looked at the war widow, mourning the loss of her beloved husband. There was a bloody handprint on the canvas.

Following my intuition, I ran my fingers over the frame until I heard a click. The painting opened like a door, exposing a secret passage in the castle.

I was too invested to turn back now. So I walked into the passage and searched for blood. The painting swung shut, as a shiver traveled down my spine.

I followed the passage to a beacon of light. And then I spotted a bloody footprint.

It looked like a basement. I walked into the room and paid attention to my surroundings. There were tables and bookcases. Jars filled with remedies.

I thought I heard someone breathing. I peeked around the bookcase and kept walking. Despite my better judgement, I plunged deeper into the circle of hell.

A crippled man turned around who looked like something had eaten his flesh. There were holes in his face, and he was humped over. But I'd recognize him anywhere.

"Tony," I gasped. "How are you alive?"

"Hello." It was scary just to look at him.

In prison, his syphilis must have gone untreated. I'd researched the symptoms when I first heard of his diagnosis. Over time, the disease was debilitating. He was close to dying.

"You know, I've often wondered why it is God has let me live so long." He moved towards me. "He should have taken me months ago. But he just won't."

"Don't come near me." I waved the flickering candle.

"I think it's so he can punish me longer. I mean, I'm already in hell."

"Stay back!" I looked for something flammable. "Help!"

"Why are you screaming?" He touched my gown. "No one is going to hear you."

"Help!" I climbed on top of a table and screamed into a vent. "TOM!"

"Come here." He chased the open air. "Let me see that pretty face."

I remembered another key symptom. Vision loss. Inevitable blindness.

"Oh, there you are Valjean. I thought I'd lost you."

Confused, I racked my brain but couldn't remember anything about hallucinations.

And then I saw him. Just on the verge of stepping into the light. It was Thin Man.

"TOM!" I screamed. "HELP!"

Valjean stalked towards me, slick as a cat. I remembered seeing him at the commemoration ceremony. Now I realized, he'd been staking out the museum.

"Where is the real necklace?" he spat, wrapping his hand around my throat.

I gagged, but managed to get a few words out. "I don't know... talking about."

"The real emerald?" he pressed. "Worn by Marie Antoinette. This isn't it."

Valjean took the necklace out of his pocket and tossed it at me. I looked at the emerald, noting the cut and clarity. It was beautiful. It always had been.

"Where is it?" He tightened his grip at my throat. "Tell me!"

When I couldn't say, he tossed me on the ground. My head hit the stone, and I felt dizzy. But I mustered the strength to sit up straight with my back to the wall.

"Hugh is still in prison," DeMilo said. "So I hired this one to help me out."

"The real emerald harvests an elixir." Valjean pointed at the stone. "And it will cure any affliction known to man. The man who possesses the stone controls the fate of the world."

"It's a lie," I coughed. "There is no such thing."

"Not a lie," Valjean snapped. "I'll prove it to you."

"It's not in here," DeMilo said. "It's always in the hands of an old man."

As they closed in on me, I lit the sleeve of my robe with the candle. Once it caught on fire, I jumped out of the robe and threw it on them. DeMilo got tangled in the flames, running for the exit. Before he could make it, someone shot him in the back.

I sank down to the floor, not knowing who might get the next bullet.

Valjean crept around the edge of the room. And someone shot him in the back. He flew out the window and landed on the concrete. Did that mean I was next?

Edmond stepped into the light with a pistol in his hand. And when DeMilo showed signs of life, Edmond shot him again. He bled out on the stone floor and I shivered.

"Are you all right?" Edmond put the gun down. "I'm not going to hurt you."

I broke down in tears as he took me in his arms. It felt so good to be held.

"I'm sorry about before. I was angry. I didn't know how else to protect you."

"I love you, Uncle Edmond. And I know my grandmother did, too."

He wiped my tears with his thumb. "She was the best sister any man could have."

"I wish I could have known her," I sobbed.

"You're a lot like her," he said. "You just don't know it yet."

I smiled despite my tears. "Valjean said the necklace was a fake."

Edmond pursed his lips.

"Was he right?" I asked.

Edmond picked the necklace up off the ground. "What do you think?"

"I don't know. I don't think I'd be able to tell the difference."

"I knew someone might steal it, so I had a replica made."

"So it is fake?"

He nodded.

"What about the other stuff Valjean said?" I

wondered.

"What did he say?"

"He said the real necklace possesses an elixir than can heal any affliction known to man. But that can't be true. That's fantasy."

"It's not fantasy, dear. It's science."

I lifted my brow at him.

"That's what makes the necklace so valuable. And that's why everyone wants it. Emeralds aren't even worth as much as diamonds. You're smart. Think about it."

"So what's inside that necklace?" I pointed at the decoy.

"Something a brilliant chemist of mine made up."

I cocked my head to the side.

"Poison."

"Addie!" Tom yelled.

I looked into Edmond's eyes—emerald green. Just like mine.

"Addie!"

I looked up as Tom came through the secret passage—the same way I had. He crashed into me, so out of breath I thought he might faint. He touched my face and kissed me.

"I thought I lost you, baby." He squeezed my arms. "I was so scared."

Edmond cleared his throat, and I looked over at him. He opened a panel in the wall and exposed a jewel safe. He twisted the dial on the front, not minding if either of us saw the combination. I clung to Tom and held my breath. I had no idea what to expect.

The real emerald necklace hung in a chilled glass case. It almost looked like a fish tank. Edmond unlocked it and took the necklace off its hook. Then he brought it over.

"Apart from family, this was your grandmother's most prized possession. You are the last living heir to the emerald necklace, Addie. Do with it what you will."

He put the necklace in the palm of my hand and closed my fingers over it.

"The choice is yours."

I gaped at the emerald as he walked away. It felt cold in my hand.

"Genevieve is here," Edmond said. "Why don't you come upstairs and she can tell you all about it?"

I nodded as he left us in peace. Tom noticed DeMilo on the floor for the first time. It might have taken him a little while to spot him. Nowadays, he was hard to recognize.

"I'm sorry, Tom." I put my hand on his shoulder. "I know he was your family."

"No, he's not." He lifted my face. "You're my family now."

We kissed and then made our way out of there. Everyone was awake by the time we reached the main floor. Ashton was yawning, and Juliette looked hungover. But I was happy to find all of my family alive. Especially once Edmond called the police.

Adeline kept nodding off on the staircase, but I had no intention of going back to sleep now. I was too wound up to climb beneath the sheets. And I planned on giving the police a full account of what happened as soon as they arrived.

"Hey, kid." Jimmy patted my shoulder. "Nothing is ever boring around you two."

Tom chuckled. "You could say that."

Genevieve walked in the front door with a stack of files. She'd been bringing archives into the castle from the car outside. I couldn't wait to hear what she'd uncovered.

I grabbed her arm so I could introduce her to Jimmy. They hadn't met yet.

But Jimmy beat me to it. When he saw her face, he looked like he'd seen a ghost.

"Josette?" He stared, gaping at her.

I looked into her eyes and covered my mouth. They looked like mine.

Edmond touched her shoulder. "I thought it was about time you met your daughter."

I looked at Ashton. I looked at Juliette. I looked at Adeline.

"You knew, didn't you?" I cried. "All of you."

Beside myself, I ran out of the castle and straight into the snow. I was barefoot and freezing without a jacket. But the cold isn't what stung. It was her betrayal.

My mother. Josette. She'd been alive all along. Living right here in France.

She left me. She abandoned me. She gave me up.

I hated her.

Running for the trees, I watched my breath crystallize in front of me.

"Addie!" Tom yelled. "Addie, come back! Please!"

He was coming after me. He always did. But I didn't want him to.

So I kept running until I found the river. It had completely frozen over days ago. And it was the same one Adeline had talked about ice skating on. Even she was a traitor.

"Addie." I heard the cock of a gun. "Give me the necklace."

I turned around to face Valjean. He was limping on his leg, and there was blood running down his shirt. Even his face looked broken and busted. But he was alive.

"Just hand it over."

I opened my hand and there it was. What everyone wanted.

"No." I took a step back, getting dangerously close to the ice.

"I almost died stealing that necklace. It belongs to me."

"No it doesn't." I walked backwards, stepping on the frozen river.

It was painfully cold. So much so, that I felt it in my bones.

In the distance, I saw Tom running towards us

with Edmond. He had a gun.

"It's over, Valjean," I said, exercising my power. "Give it up."

He knelt down on the snow in surrender. But then he lifted the pistol and aimed it right at me. Edmond shot him in the neck, but not before Valjean pulled the trigger.

It knocked the breath out of me.

I stumbled back and fell through the ice. And when I screamed, the pain amplified.

I was too weak to fight, too weak to pull myself up.

I saw the emerald necklace sinking in a circle of my own blood.

And when I shut my eyes, it all went away.

Carpe Diem

Tom

I felt Addie slipping out of my grasp. And that was the moment I should have realized that life—and every part of it I'd planned up until this point—was essentially over.

She ran outside in her bare feet like a little girl. No jacket. No shoes.

All I wanted was to bundle her up in my arms. I could keep her warm.

My grandfather's corpse was in the basement. And my wife had just escaped death at his hands for the hundredth time. That's what if felt like at least.

Maybe I was being selfish—anxious to take her away on our honeymoon. But we'd just gotten married. And I needed time with my wife. I wanted to love her and hold her.

Edmond had given her the emerald necklace.

The real one, this time.

And while I detested the damn thing, he was right about something.

Addie was the only remaining heir. It belonged to no one but her.

Until Jimmy exposed Genevieve for who she really was. Josette—Addie's biological mother. The woman she spent searching for in her dreams ever since she found Jimmy.

As much as my head was spinning, I kept the focus on Addie. She meant everything to me. And I couldn't bear the thought of another parental figure causing her grief.

But Addie was known for running away. She'd done it before our very first kiss. And I'd chased her beyond the pine trees. Because I had to taste her pretty soft lips.

I had to know that the girl I'd been pining after wasn't a pipe dream. I had to feel her and touch her. I had to believe she was real. I'd never imagined she'd actually be mine.

My body ached to comfort her. Why couldn't she run to me?

Apart from Jimmy, I was the only one in the castle who hadn't known about Genevieve. Josette, I mean. I wondered if that was the real reason Edmond had invited us here.

While Jimmy sent daggers at Josette, I went out the back door and chased Addie. She ran in the snow wearing nothing but her nightgown. "Addie!" I called out to her.

But she was so stubborn. And the more I pushed, the farther she pulled away.

And that's when I saw him. A tall lanky man approaching my girl. He had a gun.

"ADDIE!" My feet kept sinking in the snow. But I would get to her. I had to.

In no time, Edmond appeared beside me with a weapon of his own.

"Stay put." He lifted his rifle, while I thought about his years as a hunter. Before we came to Paris, Addie went on and on about the biography she'd read. Despite his being an excellent marksman, my stomach was constricting in knots. I could barely breathe.

Addie stood on the frozen river with the necklace in the palm of her hand.

Edmond fired and the man went down. But the damage was already done. Addie staggered back and fell through the ice. My whole world imploded in three seconds.

"NO!" I ran through the wilderness and jumped in the river after her. The water was so cold it shocked my heart. I thought my eyes might freeze, but I kept them open.

I saw her golden hair and plunged deeper. There were splotches of blood in the water. Droplets that moved like plasma—ebbing and flowing in a liquid rhythm.

It was her blood. And when I realized that, there wasn't much left to fear.

I grabbed her in my left arm and swam with

my right. When we surfaced, I pulled her onto the riverbank opposite the dead man. And that was when the panic started to set in.

It must have been less than a minute, but she was already so cold. I put my lips on hers and performed CPR. I would breathe for her for the rest of my life if I had to.

She coughed up a little water. Not enough to cause concern. And then she was breathing again. Her eyes opened, and I gazed into those pools of fiery green.

"Tom," she mouthed.

"I'm here." I touched her cheek. "I'll never leave you. I'm here."

She touched her side. And that's when I saw the pool of blood in the snow.

In the time it took me to get to her, he'd managed to fire more than once. One of the bullets had scraped the surface—a mere flesh wound. But the second pierced her stomach.

She looked into my eyes. And we both knew.

"It's okay." She rubbed my face. "Don't be afraid."

"No!" I held her in my arms. "No, I'm not letting you go."

"I'm so tired," she sighed. "Don't you feel tired?"

"No, baby. Stay with me. Stay with me, dammit!"

Edmond jumped in the river and swam to us. "Take your shirt off."

I did what he said, and he pushed her gown up to her chest.

"Help me lift her." He tied my shirt around her torso very tightly. "I've already called for help. Keep applying pressure to the wound. They'll be here any minute now."

Edmond stroked the side of her face in affection. "Hang in there, sweet girl."

She smiled even though she'd started to cry. When he left, I started to cry too.

"I'm really glad..." she fought through her words "...that we decided to get married."

"So am I." I gently rocked her in my arms. "Carpe diem, right?"

She laughed, and a pool of blood gushed onto my hand.

"Oh god, baby. Don't leave me. Please. Hold on."

She shivered as her skin turned glacial and white as a ghost.

"All I ever wanted was you," she whispered. "I love you. I always have."

"Baby, don't talk like that." I touched her hair. "You're so young. And we're gonna go to Italy on our honeymoon. And Jeanine will be so jealous we left her out."

She cracked a fragile smile.

"And we're gonna make lots of babies. Five minimum."

"Are you tryin' to kill me?" she muttered.

I weaved my fingers through hers. "Just keep

talking to me."

"Tom?" She had a faraway look in her eyes. "I feel cold."

I didn't want to look, but I had to. She was losing too much blood.

"I'll keep you warm, baby." I rubbed her arms. "I'll keep you warm."

"What is happening to me?" she slurred.

"Nothing. You're fine. You're gonna be just fine. Okay?"

"Last night was perfect. I wish you could hold me like that forever."

"I will, baby. I will. I promise. Just stay with me for a little while longer."

"No one ever looks at the stars at night." She closed her eyes. "They're so bright."

The blood was seeping out of her, and I didn't know what to do.

"Addie!" The tears were coming so fast I couldn't see. I could hardly make her out.

She was a blur.

"The necklace." It was her last request. "Find the necklace."

"Who cares about that damn necklace, Addie? It's not worth your life!"

An ambulance arrived in record time. I had Edmond and his nobility to thank for that.

I carried her across the river and ran to the medical truck with her in my arms. They strapped her on a gurney and rolled her into the back of the truck. She looked up at me.

Addie was in critical condition, so they wouldn't let me go with her.

"Please, I'm her husband." I grabbed the arm of the medical responder. She looked back at me in confusion. "Ma femme." I pointed at Addie and then showed her my ring.

By some miracle, they let me on. There was a man administering the oxygen who spoke English. They did their best to control the bleeding and yelled at the driver to hurry.

We passed a swarm of police cars headed to the castle. If only they'd come sooner.

"She's my wife," I cried. "I love her. We got married yesterday."

The medical team looked at me in horror.

"Please, tell me. Is she going to make it?"

The man and woman looked at each other.

"Mon amour. Mon monde," I sobbed.

"I don't know," he said. "I'm sorry. I just don't know."

"It could go either way. She's as likely to live as to—"

"No." I shook my head 'til I thought I'd lost my mind. "She can't. Not now. Not after everything we've been through." I took her hand and squeezed it. "Promise me you will do everything in your power to save her." They hesitated. "Promise me!"

"Oui monsieur." He looked me in the eye. "I promise."

I held her small hand in both of mine. And

then I sang to her. At this point, I didn't care if the whole country thought I was insane. I softly crooned every song I'd ever covered. Those intimate nights with just her and my guitar in my bedroom back home.

I'd give anything to be there now. In the past. When she was still safe.

"Blood transfusion is highly likely," he said. "Do you know her blood type?"

"I don't know."

We came to an abrupt stop as the driver pulled into the hospital. The double doors flew open, and Addie lay on the gurney unconscious. They wheeled her through the front entrance, while I struggled to keep up. Everything was so chaotic and loud.

Eventually, we reached an area where I was not allowed. A team of nurses had to hold me back to keep me from breaking down the door. When Addie was out of sight, I sank to the floor and cried. Then I squeezed the wedding band on my finger and reminisced.

It had been the perfect wedding day. The perfect wedding night.

I thought about her lips on my stomach as she kissed her way down my torso. Now the memory stung—it was almost too painful to bear. And I squeezed my eyes with tears.

Edmond found me on the floor in the hallway. He took a seat beside me. And I was surprised when he didn't say anything for a while. He was letting me get it all out.

I really appreciated that.

"Why don't you hold on to this for her?" He slipped the emerald necklace into my hand discretely. "Keep it safe. That's the only way to keep her safe."

He got up and walked away.

"Who jumped in to get it?" I asked.

"I did." Even after the drive over, his hair and clothes were still damp.

"I can't lose her," I confessed. "Nothing makes sense without her."

"Then don't," he said. "Protect the necklace. And it will protect her."

I furrowed my brow as he walked away. I didn't understand it, but maybe I didn't need to. So I cradled the emerald in my hands and prayed that everything would be all right.

She was the most beautiful girl I'd ever seen. And I'd spent most of my life loving her.

So I would plant myself right here in the hospital hall. I had nowhere else to go.

Addison was my home, my wife. And if she went, I couldn't put her in a pine box.

I couldn't bury her beneath the Savannah soil.

If she left, I would go with her.

Nothing could keep us apart. Not even death. Because she was a precious soul, a rare jewel, a gemstone. An emerald whose spirit held the elixir of life—an everlasting cure.

I eyed the emerald in my hand. It was like

looking into her eyes.

The best night of my life had been followed by the worst. But the necklace was keen on balance. It had drawn the best and worst into my life— Addie and her ambivalent fate.

I'd never been able to pin it down. Why my parents had died so young? Why I had no family? Why I'd lost everyone I'd ever loved in one fell swoop?

But I held the power now. Addie would come back to me. She had to.

Because I had her heart cradled in the palm of my hand.

Tell Me Your Favorite Part!

If you enjoyed Pearl White, I invite you to head over to Amazon and let me know your favorite part. Reviews are so important to an author's career, because they help new readers like you discover the book. Even if you didn't enjoy Pearl White, I'd still love it if you could take three minutes to let me know what you think of the book.

Leaving a review is super easy:

1) Go to Pearl White Book Page on Amazon

2) Scroll Down and click "Write a Customer Review"

3) Sign in to Amazon if prompted

4) Select a star rating

5) Write a few short words (or long words, I won't judge)

6) Click the 'submit' button

I thank you in advance!

Acknowledgements

Thank you to my close family and friends. Your encouragement means the world to me. And you inspire and uplift me every day. Don't know where I'd be without you!

Since there are too many to count, I'd like to give a huge shout-out to my fellow authors. I love working and collaborating with you all. To the authors who've inspired me throughout my life (there are also too many to count) thank you for your stories. They have influenced the writer I've become, and I can never thank you enough for that.

Thanks to my Launch Team—Lindsay's Lucky Stars. I'm so grateful to know each and every one of you. You make my job as an author well worth the writer's block.

I'd also like to thank Itsy Bitsy Book Bits and Kylie's Fiction Addiction, as well as the countless bloggers who I've come in contact with. Thank you for promoting good content on your platforms. I've discovered some of my favorite romance novels, thanks to you. And you're dedication and loyalty to independent authors will never be forgotten.

Most importantly, I'd like to thank you. Yes, you, the reader! Without readers, none of this would be possible. From the bottom of my heart, I'd like to sincerely thank you for checking out my work. You'll never know how much it means to me that there are people living all over the world who are reading my books. I can't even wrap my head around that one! But that just shows how amazing you are. Thank you for the eternal love and support. It's readers like you who make me so happy to write love stories every day. So thank you.

Happy Reading x

Lindsay

About the Author

Lindsay Marie Miller was born and raised in Tallahassee, Florida, where she graduated from high school as Valedictorian. At sixteen, she started writing her first novel, *Emerald Green*, after being inspired by Stephenie Meyer's International Bestselling *Twilight Saga*. During her time in college, Lindsay wrote 5 more novels and over 100 songs. After graduating Summa Cum Laude from Florida State University, she put her B.A. in English Literature to good use and published her debut novel, *Emerald Green*. An author of over 10 Romance Titles, Lindsay currently resides in her hometown of Tallahassee where she is always working on her next novel.

To learn more, please visit:

www.lindsaymariemillerauthor.com

Sign up for Lindsay's newsletter:

lindsaymariemillerauthor.com/claim-your-free-book/

Join Lindsay on Facebook at:

facebook.com/LindsayMarieMillerAuthor

Follow Lindsay on Twitter at:

twitter.com/Lindsay_MMiller

Here's a sneak peek of

ME & MR. JONES,

a sexy forbidden romance.

*A*nd Cain talked with Abel his brother: and it came to pass, when they were in the field, that Cain rose up against Abel his brother, and slew him … the Lord saith unto him, Therefore whosoever slayeth Cain, vengeance shall be taken on him sevenfold. And the Lord set a mark upon Cain, lest any finding him should *kill* him.

Genesis 4:8, 15

Part I
The Golden Boy

Chapter 1

I saw him before he saw me. It was cold, wet, winter, actually, and I'd come to campus without a jacket or umbrella. He walked with a smoother stride than I ever had, up ahead on the brick pathway leading to the dining hall. It was college, so I could care less who saw me staring. There were too many people around for just one to remember.

Looking down at my sneakers, I followed the pathway, already embarrassed by the squishing sound I knew they would make once I entered the classroom. It was the first day of class since winter break. And even though I already had one semester under my belt, it felt like a curse to still be considered a freshman.

I had finally declared a major: Psychology. But once I learned of the experiments that we would have to not only conduct, but participate in, my introverted nature began to cringe. I was blatantly shy, and happily so, though the subtlest bit of focus in my direction made my cheeks blush scarlet red. It tended to bring attention to the sparsely scattered freckles at the apples of my cheeks and along the bridge of my nose. They matched the dark brown hue of my hair and eyes, no matter how finite the tiny dots seemed.

After sidestepping a few mud puddles, I looked up, and he was gone. I felt a strange surge of disappointment overwhelm me. Though I had lost nothing, it somehow felt that way.

In a hurry to make it to class on time, I skidded along the last section of the brick walkway leading to the psychology department. As I fell to the slick ground, the $200 textbook, that I had been nestling beneath my arms, slipped out from under them and came crashing down, into a soupy puddle of mud.

"NO!" I yelled aloud, devastated. All I could think about was that book.

Already on my knees, I leaned over the wet pool of rainwater and picked the book up by the edge of its front cover, because that was the only way I could manage to grasp it. But the book was too heavy to lift by its front cover, so the hardbound text slid from my fingers once again, returning to the puddle with a loud, offensive splash that coated my face with dark, tepid rainwater.

"You need some help?"

Just as I began to wipe the water from my face, I looked up, and there he was. The same tall, blonde, blue-eyed image of the perfect golden boy. He must have been a senior. I could tell that much from the mature bone structure of his face. He certainly didn't look eighteen.

"No, I'm fine," I murmured. My cheeks should have turned scarlet by now, surely, if not for the murky puddle drops on my face. Of all the days I had chosen not to bring an umbrella.

"Freshman?" He squatted down before me, balancing himself around the perimeter of the puddle.

"Yeah," I admitted, quickly averting my eyes from his.

He was dressed in formal clothing: a pale blue button-down shirt and navy slacks. I imagined him on the set of a fragrance commercial for Ralph Lauren, riding horses and drinking champagne. I watched him curiously, when he unbuttoned the sleeve around his right wrist and rolled the material up to his elbow.

He looked like he had lived in California.

He looked like he had been lifting very heavy weights.

He looked like he had outgrown this place a long time ago.

So what was he doing here?

Without a second's hesitation, he stuck his hand into the filthy water and grabbed my textbook. I snapped out of my daydream, practically in a daze when he motioned for me to follow him under the shelter that extended outward from the entrance to the psychology building.

"Open your bag," he requested, pointing to the

satchel over my shoulder. Once I did, he removed a brand new psychology textbook from the backpack he was carrying and placed it in my bag.

"What are you-?" I stopped myself at the sight of him shaking out my filthy, wet textbook under the dry shelter.

"You use mine, and I'll use yours," he offered, cracking a crooked smile. I shook my head in confusion, distracted by the crystal clear look of his blue eyes. They managed to reflect the tiniest bit of light, despite the lack of sun.

"But I-"

"You could just say thank you," he boldly suggested. I wasn't used to this.

"Thank you." I glanced down at the shiny new textbook in my bag, still in disbelief. He smiled, then walked towards the entrance to the psychology department. "Wait," I called, relieved when he stopped and looked back at me. "You're not a freshman. Are you?"

"No," he answered, holding my gaze, "I'm not."

"Well," I stalled, thinking of something else to say. I didn't want the conversation to end. "Why are you so dressed up?"

"I have a presentation," he said. His tone remained somber, professional even, despite the slightest hint of a playful smirk at the corner of his mouth. I wondered how often he looked at other girls like that.

"Oh," was all I could manage. I glanced down

at his shiny black dress shoes, doubting that they would squeak as loudly as my sneakers would once I entered the building. "Well, good luck." I gazed into his beautiful, clear, liquid blue eyes and admired the seamlessly sculptured face around them, in case I should never see him again. Surely, fate couldn't be so cruel, after being so kind.

"You too," he replied, before opening the glass door and stepping inside.

Once the image of him had vanished, I entered the building in search of a bathroom. Fortunately, I was able to dry off in there with no one else gawking at me. All the stalls were empty, and I was the only one at the sinks.

My first class was on the fourth floor, so I headed upstairs in search of room 481. When I reached that level, I found the classroom just around the corner, at the end of the hallway. Anxious with the first-day-back jitters, I opened the door and hurried inside. As the door slammed shut behind me, I noticed that I had come through the front entrance of the classroom, which meant that over a hundred people were now staring at me.

Thankfully, the classroom floor was covered in dingy, gray carpet, so my shoes didn't squeak as I searched for a seat among the crowd. There were only three seats left in the entire room, all of which were located on the front row, since that was the last place most students wanted to sit on a voluntary basis. Satisfied enough, I selected the seat in the middle and sat down between the only two chairs that remained vacant. Maybe I wouldn't have to make small talk with anyone this semester, so long as the empty seats remained empty. Just as I removed the textbook from my satchel and placed it on my desk, the thought vanished.

"Oh, did you get the book already?" a candid, feminine voice wondered. I looked up to find that the girl sitting to the left of the empty seat beside me had leaned over in curiosity.

She had a small face, green eyes, and a pile of light brown hair that she had pulled back into a messy ponytail. The ends of her hair looked a little damp, not unlike the collection of water spots on her t-shirt that appeared to be in the process of drying. I assumed that she must have forgotten an umbrella as well and immediately sought her ought as an ally.

"Yeah." I smiled, making my best attempt at polite conversation.

"Can I look at it?"

"Sure." I handed the heavy book to her. It was a fifth edition clinical psychology textbook, complete with diagrams and pull-out charts for studying.

"I heard it was really expensive." She flipped through the pages, briefly stopping when she came across a full color picture of Sigmund Freud. "How much did you get it for?"

"About two hundred," I replied, wondering if that was the actual price he had paid for it.

"That's ridiculous," she huffed. "I'm not paying that!"

I forced a laugh, only to be nice, really. Once our conversation ended, all was quiet again, so I turned around in my chair to search the classroom for familiar faces. I did not recognize a single soul.

When the door clicked open, I looked back to watch another student enter the classroom. A teenage boy with big glasses, dish water blonde tresses, and a sloppy posture walked in and sat down in the empty seat to my right. He kept his gaze down to avoid all eye contact, probably just as nervous as the rest of us were for the new semester.

Just as the door was about to swing shut, a dark shoe wedged its way through, catching the bottom of the door before it could close. When the door opened, I widened my eyes in surprise. I never would have dreamed that he would be standing in the doorway. Cool and confident, the golden boy entered the classroom, gracing me with his presence for the second time today. I immediately straightened up in my chair, anxiously anticipating him. The only remaining seat was the one next to mine, and I knew he would have to take it.

I cocked my head to the side when his feet moved in an unexpected direction, and he set his backpack down on the large desk at the front of the classroom. What was he doing?

Noticing me in the front row, he smiled in my direction, his blue eyes twinkling with delight.

Before I could comprehend what was going on, he opened his mouth and began.

"Hey guys," he greeted, waving a strong, manly hand in the air. "Welcome back. My name is Cabel Jones, and I'll be your instructor for this course. Any questions before we get started today?"

Chapter 2

After overcoming the initial shock of who he was, I could still feel the warm blood of my blushing cheeks, that had lingered there for the first half of class. Cabel seemed as down-to-earth as a professor could be in the eyes of a student, talking with an air of casual confidence. I was impressed to hear that he had attended college at Northwestern University, received his master's degree at Johns Hopkins University, and then finished off with a doctorate in clinical psychology at Cornell University. As if that were not enough, his desire for scholastic achievement was so great, that he had been able to do all of this on an accelerated fast track, meaning he was still only twenty-five years old.

With the presence of this newfound knowledge came a drastically altered opinion of him. He didn't look the same anymore, not at all like the charming young golden boy I had pictured him to be. Now, he was older, wiser, and more accomplished than any other man I had met of the same age. The planes of his face were harder, his cheekbones more narrowly defined, his jawline more taut and linear. I should have noticed that his shoulders were much too broad and muscular for a senior frat boy, who spent his nights juggling women and tequila. Cabel Jones was hardly like the narrative that I had conjured up in my mind.

In fact, he was bold, brilliant, and breathtaking. But he was also ineligible. The thought settled with me for a long time. Knowing that he wasn't a student only made me wonder how things would have gone that day in the rain, if he had been.

The following day, I stopped by his office, intent on returning the book to him. Mine was destroyed, and to keep his copy all semester just didn't feel right. So, when the moment arrived, I knocked on the partially cracked door to his office and looked inside.

"Come in," he called, removing a pair of reading glasses from his face. I approached his desk at a sluggish pace, pleased to find that his looks had not changed. If I hadn't known any better, I would have believed that he was the reincarnation of James Dean.

"Do you remember me?" My words sounded awfully meek, though I couldn't really help it.

"Ah, yes." He nodded, then set his reading glasses down beside a plethora of scattered documents on his desk. "The other day in the rain."

I kept quiet, remembering how embarrassing that day in the rain had been.

"Come in," he said. "Have a seat." I silently

obeyed, hoping that I appeared as cool and collected as he did. "So, what can I help you with today?"

I took a shallow breath, then looked down at all of the pages on his desk. They had been carefully spread out, like maps for a treasure hunt. What was he looking for?

"I wanted to give you your book back." I reached into my satchel and grabbed the heavy textbook. "I know it's expensive," I admitted, "and you shouldn't have to use the one that I dropped in the water." Pleased with myself, I handed the book over his desk and waited for him to take it. Despite my innocent smile, Cabel folded his hands together and relaxed into the back of his chair. He wasn't interested.

"I don't have your book," Cabel confessed.

"Oh." I wiped the smile off my face and returned the book to my satchel. Hopefully, he wouldn't be able to make out the disappointment in my eyes.

"I recycled it," he explained. "If you had tried to take it back to the store and exchange it for another, they wouldn't have taken it." I furrowed my brow, not understanding him. "Because of all the water damage," he continued, answering my unasked questions.

"Oh, I see." My fingers clutched the satchel in my lap, nervously tugging at the fabric. I knew that the respectable thing to do was to offer to pay for the book. But I didn't have $200 lying around to cover the cost. I kept my eyes on the front wooden paneling of his desk, as I tried to think of the best way to respond. Before I could, Cabel sensed my inner struggle and spoke again.

"The publisher always sends me a few extra textbooks for every class, and I gave you one of those." I looked into Cabel's clear, liquid blue eyes while he talked. He was so young. "So, feel free to keep it," he offered. "I usually hand them out to students anyway, so it's no problem." Cabel toyed with the arms of his reading glasses, momentarily distracting me.

"All right," I agreed with a smile. "Thank you, Professor. I mean, Mr. Jones, er, Dr. Jones? I mean..." I closed my eyes in embarrassment, running a hand through my dark locks to ease my bewilderment. My heart rate increased, as I contemplated whether or not I had just displayed a lack of respect towards the man who would be administering my final grade.

He merely chuckled. The deep timbre of his voice stirred something within me that miraculously cooled my blood, if only for an instant. "Cabel's fine," he insisted. "I'm not much older than most of you, so there's no need to act like it."

All I could manage was a perpetual nod, until he changed the subject.

"So, have you signed up for the first experiment yet?" He leaned forward, folding his hands over the surface of his desk. I imagined that in thirty years, he would continue to age gracefully, like Robert Redford or Paul Newman. I hoped the blonde wouldn't fade.

"Yes," I breathed. "Mine is at 9:30 a.m. on Friday."

"Good," he mentioned, nodding his head with approval. "We'll have six more after this one, so make sure you pay close attention. Will this be your first experiment?"

"Yes, do you know what it will be about?" I couldn't help wondering.

"The topics should be posted sometime today, but the first one is normally pretty mellow, as far as intensity is concerned. It shouldn't be anything to worry about." He pressed his lips together, forming a thin, fine line. "Now, you've taken the prerequisite for this course, correct?"

"Yeah, I took it last semester, in the fall. That's the only prerequisite for the course, right?"

"Yes." He put his reading glasses back on and picked up one of the documents from his desk. "But this is an upper-level course, so be prepared, because it's going to take a lot more time and work than your lower-level courses."

"Okay." I slipped my satchel over my shoulder and rose from the chair, ready to leave. "Well, thanks for your help." I headed for the door, slightly offended that he had denounced my capabilities as a student, simply because I was a freshman.

"What is your name?" he asked, while I

lingered in the doorway.

"Finley," I briefly announced, surprised that he had cared to ask.

"Finley?" His piercing blue eyes held my gaze, contemplating and watching.

"O'Connell. Finley O'Connell," I reiterated, merely for clarification's sake.

"Well, Miss O'Connell, I look forward to having you in my class this semester." He grabbed a pencil from a glass jar resting on his desk and returned to his work, noticeably unaffected. I silently turned away, not knowing what else to say.

"Oh, and Miss O'Connell?" he called after me, just as I placed my hand on the doorknob.

I looked back at him one last time, wondering how I would make it through the semester with a James Dean/Robert Redford/Paul Newman look-alike as my professor.

"Stay dry."

Chapter 3

When Friday morning came, I felt a rumbling of butterflies in my stomach, as I headed towards the psychology building for my first experiment. I was told to wait in the lobby on the third floor, where fifteen other students were already fidgeting in their chairs, anxious to have the experiment over. One by one, each of them was called away by a young woman with a clipboard, who politely led them down the corridor and out of my sight. Within no time, I was the only one left.

Jittery, I rose from my seat and paced the length of the room, looking through a pair of wide windows. I spotted a handful of students on the brick walkway, down below, shouting and giggling, as they hurried off to class.

"Finley O'Connell." The young woman with the clipboard appeared, pen in hand.

"Yes." I clutched the satchel that I had been carrying over my shoulder and turned around with a smile on my face. I was prepared to walk down that long corridor and finally know what they were going to do to me.

"I'm afraid that your experimenter wasn't able to make it today," the young woman said. I felt my brow furrow in confusion, as I watched her scribble something onto a small notepad, before tearing a strip of paper from it. "Here." She handed the note to me. "You're still receiving full credit for the experiment today. That's our policy when the experimenter doesn't show up." She glanced down at her clipboard again, and then checked my name off the lengthy list.

"Oh." I studied the note in my hand. She had written down the amount of credit that the experiment was worth, and then signed her initials beside it. "Well, thank you." I shrugged, feeling each wave of nervous energy slowly lift away.

By the time I made it to class, most of the students were already there, discussing the various experiments they had just participated in. I grabbed my chair in the front row and sat down, unable to keep from eavesdropping on all of the others.

"They made me put my hand in this box and then I had to hit this button," one girl said. "Most of the time it did nothing, but every now and then, it would shock my hand." I leaned back in my seat and angled my body towards her, so I could listen. "I hated it," she cringed.

"Didn't they tell you what they were going to do?" the guy beside her wondered.

"Not until right before," she replied. "They made me sign a disclaimer too."

"We all have to do that," he declared, taking a tone with her. "All I had to do was watch some video, and then they made me answer questions."

"That's it?" the girl whined, scowling in frustration. "Lucky! That's so not fair," she griped, forcing an incredibly loud sigh from her lips.

I turned around in my chair and sat up straight, looking down at the textbook on my desk. Despite what Cabel had told me, the experimenting process was not going to be as relaxed as I had originally thought. I certainly wasn't looking forward to having my pain threshold tested, should that be the topic I received.

Typically, experiment topics were posted with a brief description at least a few days before the experiment date. But the faculty had just passed a new rule, which allowed them to conduct experiments without the participants knowing which topics they would be selected for. This was supposed to increase the validity of each individual experiment, since there was no possible way to form any biases or predispositions beforehand. If no one knew the nature of the experiment, then how could the results be anything but accurate?

We had all begun an unexpected game of Russian roulette.

I just hoped that I wasn't the first to get the bullet.

* * *

That night, I stopped by the grocery store to pick up a few things for the apartment. I was running low on food and would need plenty to survive my dull, study-filled weekend. How I longed to be one of those college students who could party and drink without a care in the world, while their grades staggered and their inhibitions dissolved. Wasn't it fun to feel that free? I would never know, and for that reason, I had always told myself that all the fun was overrated.

As I trailed through the grocery store, my eyes glazed over a selection of exotic fruits, imported from Brazil. I shook my head at the obscene price for one package of sliced mango. These were obviously not the delicacies reserved for my budget, so I waltzed over to the dairy section in anticipation. Finally, something with mass appeal.

A family of four created a wall in front of me, slowing the pace of my hurried strides. My patience wore thin, while I followed their languid footsteps to the dairy section. Once they grabbed a few packages of cheese and left, I breathed a sigh of relief and scanned the shelves before me. A familiar face caught the corner of my eye, as I turned to find Cabel reaching for a carton of milk.

Panicking, I froze in place, then began walking backwards until I nearly collided with an elderly man on a motorized cart. "Sorry," I whispered to the man.

He looked me up and down, glaring as he

increased the speed of his motorized cart. "Teenagers," he huffed, then zipped away. You would have thought he was racing for NASCAR.

Thankfully, Cabel was still scanning the countless shelves of dairy items when I looked back at him. He hadn't noticed my scuffle with Jeff Gordon, so I still had time to make a break for it. As I turned on my heel, the family of four returned with their sloth-like pace. In a frenzy, I dodged the children, sidestepped a few soccer moms, and nearly collided with another cart-riding senior citizen, until I crashed into a display table, where an employee had just filled a tray with small, translucent cups of orange soda, to be handed out as free samples.

The table collapsed, barely missing the employee, as the samples toppled over, sending a wave of orange foam across the floor. I lay there, in a gushing river of cold soda, with the overturned table to my back. My hair and clothing were soaking wet, dripping from the sweet, carbonated beverage. I shut my eyes, exhaled, and tried to imagine a scenario that could have been more embarrassing. *Well*, I thought to myself, *you could have been naked.*

"Miss O'Connell?"

My eyes shot open in alarm. There he stood, the golden boy, towering over me with his beautiful blonde hair, light blue eyes, and muscle tone. Did he always look like he had just walked off the set of a movie? With the right lighting,

Cabel could have passed for a Brad Pitt body double.

"Mr. Jones," I squeaked, unable to hide my humiliation.

"Cabel," he corrected, offering an outstretched hand.

"Right." I placed my hand in his and let him pull me to my feet. "Thanks."

In a hurry to run and hide, I stepped around the orange stream of syrupy liquid. But the movement was a slippery one, as my shoes slid over the linoleum floor. Before I had the chance to fall, Cabel grabbed my waist and pulled me towards him. I felt his arms at the small of my back, supporting my shaky balance, while my hands found his shoulders.

"Are you okay?" he asked.

I nodded, feeling a sense of sadness wash over me, when he withdrew his arms.

"Here you go." The employee who had been serving samples of orange soda handed me a towel, and then dropped a yellow CAUTION sign onto the messy floor.

"Thank you." I took the towel from her and began the rushed process of drying off. "And I'm sorry," I added, just as she knelt down to wipe up the mess.

"It's okay." She smiled, then returned to her work.

Cabel grabbed my elbow and pulled me away from the scene, while I dried my hair off with the towel. We stopped to talk in the next aisle, where no one was handing out free samples.

"So tell me, Miss O'Connell," he chuckled. "Why is it that I can never seem to catch you out of the rain?" Immediately taking offense, I looked into his eyes and glared. Maybe Cabel was the pompous frat boy after all. He certainly looked it in his thin t-shirt and jeans.

"For a professor, you sure do act like a student," I boldly declared.

Cabel's mouth dropped open as he took a step back, unable to believe what I had just said. I could hardly believe it myself, but at least he knew what it felt like to be slighted now. I shook the rest of the orange liquid from my clothing and handed him the towel, which he quietly accepted. Frustrated, I ignored the disappointed look in his eyes and walked off, headed for the exit.

* * *

On Monday morning, I trudged to class with a sour expression on my face. I couldn't imagine what Cabel must think of me or what he was going to say. Why couldn't I be one of those students who skipped class every now and then? If I were, I wouldn't be worried about the look on Cabel's face when I walked through the door, because I would still be sleeping through my alarm. Why did I have to care so much?

When I reached the fourth floor of the psychology building, I spotted Cabel in the hallway and froze. He looked up at the sight of me and approached, as a sudden wave of nausea pulsed through my stomach. "Miss O'Connell," he summoned.

I lifted my head and looked up, into his piercing blue eyes. Cabel was wearing a white dress shirt with a black-and-blue striped tie, as well as a pair of black dress pants and shoes. I couldn't help thinking he looked handsome.

"Stop by my office after class," he instructed. "There's something we need to discuss."

I took a deep breath and nodded, but said nothing. Cabel opened the door to our classroom and let me inside, acting like a proper gentleman. Worry flooded through me as I made my way to the front row, because I knew what he wanted to talk about.

Why had I been so snippy at the grocery store? After all, he was my professor. Wasn't I supposed to treat him with the utmost respect? But that was just it. Cabel wasn't some sixty-five-year-old Nobel Laureate with tenure and an impending retirement. In fact, he wasn't much older than me. He had said so himself.

I avoided Cabel all throughout the lecture, too afraid to meet those light, icy blue eyes, afraid that he would be able to see into my soul, my fears, my past. When class was finished, I collected my things and left my seat in a hurry, already worrying about what he had planned for the two of us to discuss.

I headed downstairs and stayed in the main lobby for about ten minutes, not wanting to face the inevitable. What was he going to do? Kick me out of his class for being rude on Friday night? Surely, that couldn't be a rule. Could it?

Tired of stalling, I cast my fears aside and took the elevator up to Cabel's office, too shaky for the stairwell. When I arrived at his half-open door, I didn't even have to knock.

"Come in, Miss O'Connell," he beckoned.

Breathless, I swallowed my pride and walked into the room.

Chapter 4

Before taking a seat, I glanced around Cabel's office and observed how organized everything was. There was a wooden bookshelf that sat along the far right wall, whose books had been alphabetized according to separate categories and subsections of psychology. It looked like Cabel had an entire shelf dedicated to Freud and everything the man had ever researched.

His wooden desk was perfectly polished, clean, and devoid of the messy paperwork I had seen there last week. Cabel's framed diplomas hung on the wall behind him, just as straight as an arrow. Even the windows in his office were spotless, streak-free enough to fool a flying bird.

Why hadn't I noticed this before?

Curious, I sat down in the chair across from Cabel's desk and wondered just how often the term "neat freak" had been thrown his way. For years, I had heard much of the same.

"Well, Miss O'Connell," Cabel started, folding his hands over his desk. "I wanted to talk to you about-"

"I'm sorry, Mr. Jones," I interrupted. "I

shouldn't have been so rude at the grocery store." I shook my head and lowered my eyes to the floor. "I was just so embarrassed about falling down and making a fool out of myself, especially in front of you."

My cheeks flushed at the sound of my own words. What had I just said to him? *Especially in front of you?* Embarrassed, I bit my tongue and lifted my eyes to his face. To my surprise, Cabel looked just as lost as he was amused.

"Miss O'Connell, it's okay." Cabel levelled his eyes at me, turning soft, all of a sudden. "That's not why I called you in here today." I leaned back in the chair, unsure if I had heard him correctly.

"It's not?" My eyes darted from Cabel to his diplomas on the wall, and then back again.

"No." He shook his head from side to side, regarding me coolly.

"Then why did you?" I held his gaze and waited for him to scold me for interrupting, but he didn't. Instead, Cabel opened the top drawer of his desk and removed a thin yellow folder.

"So, David didn't show?" Cabel eyed me carefully, searching for truth.

"Who's David?" Was I in the Twilight Zone here? Nothing this man said made sense.

"Your experimenter," Cabel explained. "Last Friday?"

"Oh, yeah," I clarified, remembering. "But they still gave me the credit, so it's fine."

Cabel set the folder down, then leaned back in

his office chair. He placed his hands on the arms of the chair and looked at me. "Are you familiar with our new policy for experimentation?"

"Yes." I nodded. "We don't sign up for topics anymore. They are chosen at random."

"Right," he confirmed. "Now, I don't usually do this, but since you weren't able to participate in the first experiment, I will." Cabel opened the folder, collected a stapled set of papers, and handed them to me. "That's a list of all the experiments that need to be conducted this semester."

"Okay," I said, scanning the list before me. Apparently, these experiments were intended to test our limits, fears, emotional responses, and thought processes. It all seemed very standard to me. But I felt behind, now that I knew the rest of the class had completed at least one of these on the list, while I hadn't done any.

"Do you have any questions?" He leaned forward in his chair, anticipating me.

"Yes, I do." I rested the papers in my lap and gazed up at him. "What if the next experimenter doesn't show up again? I know that I'll receive the credit anyway, but I want to participate in these experiments. I want to earn the credit."

"I understand." Cabel angled his head towards me, a hidden smile straddling the edge of his lips. "I'll make sure that the next experimenter shows up," he promised. "David should know better, but I'll make sure you're placed with someone more reliable."

"Thanks." I smiled, feeling his eyes on me when I looked away. "And I am sorry," I apologized, "about last Friday." I shrugged my shoulders and stared at the ground. "There's really no excuse for it. I just wanted to apologize." When I dared to glance up at him, Cabel was smiling.

"You're shy, but only at first," he murmured.

His soft blue eyes traveled the length of my face, as I felt my cheeks blush on cue. When I widened my eyes at him, he pressed his lips together and smirked. The movement accentuated his pretty, pouty lips, though I wished it hadn't. I finally realized that having Cabel as eye candy for an entire semester of lectures was not going to be fun. This was torture.

"Thanks," I replied, not knowing what else to say. Before he could make a similar remark, I changed the subject. "I should go. My next class starts in twenty minutes." I rose from my seat and headed towards the door, but not without Cabel tacking on his two cents worth.

"Let me know if you have any problems with the next experimenter," he announced.

"Thanks, Mr. Jones." I had nearly reached the door, when he spoke again.

"When are you going to start calling me by my name?"

I stopped in my tracks and turned back to him, trying to decipher the tone of his voice. But Cabel's face had turned deadpan, expressionless.

Was he actually serious?

"That is your name," I boasted.

Cabel squared his shoulders, and then rose from his desk, clearly displeased. When he walked over to me, I felt my heartbeat escalate and my cheeks burn crimson. Cabel opened the door to his office, while I remained frozen in place, utterly perplexed by his behavior.

"Go to class," he commanded, motioning into the empty hallway. "You'll be late."

Darting my eyes to the floor, I walked out of his office and down the hall. The door slammed shut behind me, as I wondered what I had done wrong this time. Wasn't Cabel my professor? Wasn't I supposed to call him Mister? Besides, it wasn't like he had much room to talk. What was the purpose of calling me Miss O'Connell?

* * *

A couple of weeks later, I was due for the second experiment, though it was really my first. As I waited in the third floor lobby, my mind flooded with strange visions of what the experiment could entail. I remembered studying the long-term effects of child abuse, as they translated into adulthood, for the last exam. Surely, that wouldn't be a potential topic for the experiment.

I didn't want anyone delving into that part of my psyche. Ever.

As I got tangled up in my daydreams, the

remaining students were called away for their own experiments. Before too long, I was the last one left. Again. An uneasy feeling flowed through my system, because the déjà vu felt all too expected, all too planned.

Sighing aloud, I carried my satchel over my shoulder and rose from my chair in the lobby. I trudged across the carpet with my head down, desperate to go back to my apartment and sleep. Nightmares of my past had tormented me the night before, but I didn't want to revisit them now.

"Miss O'Connell," a cheery voice called. I looked up to find Cabel with a pen and clipboard in his hand. "Ready?" He turned on his heel as I followed, letting him guide me down the hallway.

"For what exactly?" I searched for the nearest elevator, intent on heading home and curling into a ball on the couch. But when Cabel grabbed my elbow, I gave him a second glance.

"Your experiment," he answered, furrowing his brow in frustration. "It's today."

"I know it's today," I snapped back, already irritated. "My experimenter didn't show up." I brushed past him and continued down the corridor, desperate to find a place to rest my head.

"I'm your experimenter." The strength of his voice followed me, traveling down the hall.

I slowed my feet and turned back around, not believing a word he had said. "What?" Cabel stepped towards me, his icy blue eyes dilating at the pupil. I thought that was odd, considering the bright fluorescent lights overhead. "Come with me," he pressed, his steady gaze authoritative and haunting, "unless you want to fail."

I forced myself to swallow, then followed Cabel down several long, winding corridors, until he finally led me into an empty room and shut the door behind us. Cabel flipped the light switch on, to reveal a small rectangular table with two wooden chairs on either side of it. I glanced around the room, spotting a couch against the left wall and a sink by the lone window at the back of the room. The blinds were drawn.

I flinched when Cabel shut the door, and then jerked one of the chairs out from the table. "Have a seat," he ordered. Obedient, I tossed my satchel onto the couch and took a deep breath.

"Yes, Mr. Jones." I sat down with my feet flat on the ground, my hands gripping the seat.

"When are you going to stop calling me that?" Cabel stood in front of me, hovering.

"When are you going to stop calling me Miss O'Connell?" I countered.

The edge of Cabel's mouth lifted into a smirk, though he didn't allow the smile to linger. I held his gaze, looking up at him through my eyelashes, playful and coy. Cabel narrowed his eyes at me in return, but not out of malice. He was thinking, wondering, considering.

"Roll up your sleeve," Cabel instructed, staring at my black long-sleeved t-shirt.

"What?" I stared up at him in confusion, while

Cabel merely sighed. All at once, he leaned forward, grabbed my left wrist with one hand, and pushed my shirtsleeve back with the other, until the fabric became a bunched mess around my elbow. I held my breath at the touch of his skin against mine, while Cabel rocked back on his heels and placed his hands on his hips.

"Put your arm on the table," he said, alarming me further. I rested my left arm on the table beside me and turned my palm up towards the ceiling. When Cabel collected a black box from the TV stand and placed it on the table, I began to sweat.

"Don't I have to sign a disclaimer first?" I piped up, questioning his order and method of experimentation.

"We'll get to that," Cabel confirmed.

Just as he unlocked the box and opened the lid, our eyes met with frantic delight. I forced myself to swallow, my gaze shifting from Cabel to the table. What was inside of the box?

Suddenly, an alarm sounded overhead, sending a violent ringing through my ears. Cabel shut the box and returned it to the TV stand, then jerked me out of the chair. Before I could react, an announcement came over the PA system.

"Attention all students, faculty, and staff. Please evacuate campus immediately. This is not a drill. Find the nearest exit and leave now. All classes are cancelled until further notice."

The announcement played on a continuous loop, while the alarm rang on and on.

"Cabel, what's going on?" I tried to swallow, but there was no more than a hard, relentless lump in my throat. Distracted, Cabel released me and moved to the door, deftly clicking the lock in place. "Cabel?" He grabbed the chair I had been sitting in and pushed it in front of the door, then snatched the table and remaining chair off the floor and did the same.

Cabel weaved his fingers through his hair, those blonde locks becoming disheveled and unruly. His head snapped back when someone began pounding their fist against the door. I looked into Cabel's eyes and noticed that his soft blue irises had thinned around two deep circles of black.

Without any warning, Cabel grabbed my arm and steered me towards the window. He drew the blinds back, and then pushed the window open to reveal our only way out.

"No!" I protested, struggling against him. Cabel grabbed my shoulders and shoved me towards the window. I stomped his foot with my shoe and kicked him in the knee, but Cabel wrapped his arm around my waist and leaned his head on my shoulder.

"Climb down the railing and go next door," he whispered. "Take the stairs to the third floor and wait for me in the second room on the left. It's the janitor's closet." I felt his warm breath in my ear, his words more comforting than the vice-like grip he had around me.

"What?" I whimpered, tugging at his arm. "But, I don't understand."

"Trust me," he pleaded in earnest.

The banging against the door only grew louder, as I tried to rationalize, tried to think, tried to decide what to do. I didn't know if I could even trust Cabel. I hardly knew him. But in that moment, I realized how badly I wanted to.

"Is this part of the experiment?" I craned my neck around to look back at him, my eyes dancing across the planes of his strong, chiseled face.

"No," he mouthed, his lips so close to mine that they nearly touched. For the briefest moment, Cabel looked at peace with the world, gazing into my fearful brown eyes. But then the door burst open, and Cabel picked me up and tossed me out the window.

Chapter 5

Bracing myself, I stuck my hands forward to weaken the impact of the fall. But when I landed on the concrete, my right ankle twisted with just enough pressure to bring tears to my eyes. I cried out in pain, clutching my ankle between my hands.

"Run!" Cabel shouted. I looked up from the flat of my back to find him leaning through the window, his hands on the railing. "Run!" he repeated, waving me towards the closest building.

Hesitant at first, I placed my palms on the cool cement, and then eased myself onto my left foot. Just as I regained my balance, a gunshot sounded overhead and Cabel's body lurched forward.

"Go," he groaned, just before they pulled him away and closed the window.

Panic-stricken, I hobbled my way to the nearest building and took the elevator to the third floor. When the doors opened, I spotted a group of men across the hall, leaving the stairwell. They all looked the same: tall, strong, armed, dressed in black shirts, shoes, pants, and masks. With my injured ankle, I didn't stand a chance.

Terrified, I stayed on the elevator and rode it to the fifth floor. When the doors opened to an empty landing, I got off in search of a place to hide. I traveled with ease, as I twisted the knob to every door, only to find that each one was locked, and I had no key to get in.

The elevator dinged, sending a slow, lingering heat through my body. On pure adrenaline, I rushed into the stairwell and watched through the window in the door, as one of the armed men stepped off. The elevator doors shut behind him, and he moved with stealth, searching the fifth floor.

Sinking to the ground, I kept my back to the stairwell door. Questions raced through my mind, as I succumbed to the fear, letting it lance through me like a knife. Where was Cabel? What had they done to him? Where were they taking him? And if they truly had taken him, then what were they going to do to me?

I listened to the elevator chime again, and then opened my eyes. When the silence remained, I mustered enough courage to lean on my left foot and look through the glass.

The man was gone.

Breathing a sigh of relief, I slowly hobbled down a flight of steps to the fourth floor. As I approached the stairwell door and looked in the window, the man appeared through the glass. Horrified, I let out the most piercing scream, and then raced up the steps on one foot. While I struggled to keep my balance, the man pushed the door open and came after me.

He grabbed my leg and dragged me down the staircase, showing no remorse when my chin slammed into one of the steps. I cried aloud, then twisted onto my back to find him standing over me with his gun aimed at my face.

Helpless, I gazed into his cold, dark eyes with every fiber of my being and willed him not to hurt me. "Please," I begged, covered in a sheen of fear and sweat. "Let me go." My lower lip trembled, as a sticky substance trickled down my chin.

I tasted the sweat.

I tasted the salt.

I tasted the blood.

"Please," I wailed, crying on the floor. "Let me go."

The man cocked his head to the side, peering down at me through his black mask. I shuddered at the sight of his chilling, callous glare, as he searched every inch of my face, weighing me, judging me, deciding whether or not I deserved to live. Then, just as calmly, he straightened his neck and uttered, "No."

Cabel burst through the stairwell door and bashed the man in the head with a fire extinguisher. The man's knees buckled and he collapsed, seemingly unconscious. I lay at the bottom of the stairs, sobbing with relief, while Cabel set the extinguisher on the ground and searched the man. When his icy blue eyes met mine, I gazed up at him in silent gratitude.

He knelt down before me and took my face in his hands. I hung my head and sobbed aloud, letting my emotions overwhelm me, as the tears multiplied. Never losing focus, he removed his tie and wrapped it around my ankle, forming a makeshift bandage. I placed my arm on his shoulder until he was finished, thankful for his gentle touch.

Quietly brooding, Cabel tucked my hair behind my ear, and then grabbed the man's gun. I watched through blurry tears, as he stood up and tucked the gun into the waistband of his pants. "We have to go," he said, gingerly taking my arm. I nodded, though kept my eyes down, while he led me to the elevator.

When we heard footsteps approaching from down the hall, Cabel picked me up, pulled me into the janitor's closet, and shut the door behind us. I squealed in pain as my right foot came down on the floor, but Cabel clamped his hand over my mouth to quiet the noise.

"Calm down," he breathed. "Are you trying to get us killed?"

As my eyes adjusted to the darkness, I was able to make out the faintest image of a mop in the corner. Except for the sliver of light beneath the door, Cabel and I were in complete blackness. I couldn't even see his face. Upset, I grabbed his wrist and peeled his hand from my mouth.

"I don't understand what's going on," I

complained. "Why won't you tell me?"

The doorknob began twisting in a wild manner, as I let out a fearful gasp of air. Cabel wrapped his arm around my stomach and pulled me to the back of the closet with him, then covered my mouth with his hand again. I tensed up when Cabel's left forearm glided over my smooth stomach, forcing the hem of my shirt up to my waist. His hand felt strange and foreign over my bare skin, though I kept my eyes straight ahead.

When the doorknob stopped rattling, I listened to the sound of my heavy breathing, as loud air blew out of my nostrils. Cabel relaxed his grip, though only slightly, to keep me wrapped in his embrace. I could feel his heart beating in quick, pounding rhythms, while my back lay flush against his chest.

Cabel rested his chin on my shoulder, as the slightest bit of stubble from his beard tickled my skin. His hot breath blew across my neck and past my ear, sending tingles down my spine. Before I could react to the sensation, a strange object rolled through the gap beneath the door and filled the room with smoke.

Chapter 6

The poisonous vapor burned my throat, clouding the entire room with thick, toxic fog. I could hardly see my own hand, much less Cabel, as the smoke continued to rise and widen. Violently coughing, I grabbed the collar of my shirt and pulled the fabric over my mouth, to prevent the gas from reaching my lungs.

"Cabel!" I yelled, reaching out for him with my other hand. "Cabel!" My eyes stung and my nostrils felt like they were on fire, but he was all I could think about. "Where are you?"

I felt Cabel's grip around my arm, as he pulled me to the ground. But the air was so thick with smoke, that I couldn't do more than wiggle within his grasp. "Come on!" he shouted, nudging me towards a patch of clear air in the floor. Confused, I eyed the smokeless hole warily, unable to understand what I was looking at.

"What?" I coughed back at Cabel, putting both hands on the floor, while my knees dug into the hard ground. Growing impatient, Cabel grabbed my hips and dropped me into the hole.

I tumbled downward, landing on a wooden

staircase with a noticeable thud. Wincing at the pain in my ankle, I slid my way down the steps and into an old, abandoned basement. Alone in the dark room, I crawled onto the floor and sat up with my back against the wall. I was definitely going to have bruises tomorrow.

Cabel fell through the trap door more gracefully, and then clambered down the steps in haste. "Are you all right?" He unfastened the top button of his white dress shirt and crouched down before me. I kept my eyes on the ground, unable to form words. My shoulders ached, as I lolled my head back against the wall, dreadfully fatigued.

"Yeah," I exhaled, tired of the pain. Anxious, I looked down at my ankle and noticed how quickly my foot had begun to swell. Cabel's black tie had come loose, and now that I had fallen down the stairs, the throbbing had only gotten worse.

Cabel refastened the tie, hurriedly wrapping the material around my ankle. I winced, though only slightly, when he knotted the tie at the heel of my foot. "I'm sorry," Cabel whispered. His hand lingered near my ankle, while his cool blue eyes scanned my face.

"At least we can breathe now," I murmured, offering the faintest of smiles.

Dust floated down from the ceiling above, as we both looked up at the sound of banging. Whoever was standing outside the janitor's closet had yet to find a way in. Determined, Cabel rose to his feet and walked towards one of the countless windows lining the far left wall.

"What are you doing?" I groaned, too concentrated on the pain to think of anything else.

"I'm getting out of here." Cabel found a stack of bricks in the corner, near the window, and picked one of them up. "Are you coming or not?" he asked.

I hesitated, eyeing him quietly from across the room. "My ankle," I explained. "I can't walk on it." I shrugged my shoulders, as if there was nothing else that either of us could do.

"So, I'll-"

"Just go and get help," I interrupted. "I'll stay here."

Beyond exhaustion, I took a deep breath and closed my eyes, not wanting to fight anymore. When I opened them, Cabel was standing over me with a look of fury on his face. I had never seen him so still.

"What?" I looked up at him, lethargic and weary. Cabel shook his head, and then placed his hands beneath my armpits, jerking me up like I was a little girl. "Ah," I sucked in a deep breath of air and scowled.

"Come on," he demanded. "I'll carry you." Cabel bent down and tucked his arm beneath my knees, while his other arm supported my back.

"Stop!" I protested, nearly losing my balance. "I don't want to be carried."

Cabel withdrew from my body, gaping at me in shock.

"Go!" I commanded. "You're wasting time!"

Cabel glared down at me, his husky blue eyes sending tingles down my spine. When he released me, I felt a twinge of disappointment, though I couldn't understand why. Cabel crossed the room, grabbed one of the bricks, and tossed it through the window. Glass shattered across the floor, as Cabel looked back at me for the last time.

I heard his feet hit the ground, after he climbed through the window and landed outside. The banging upstairs grew louder, as I lifted my face to the ceiling. Dust rained down from up above, choking and blinding me. Distressed, I turned my head back to the broken window, but Cabel was gone.

Realizing my mistake, I crawled across the floor and hobbled onto my left foot. Just as the sound of footsteps came barreling down the hidden staircase, I gritted my teeth and hurled my body through the window. The grassy ground was harder than I had anticipated, but I was thankful for the row of bushes that concealed my presence.

A car door slammed as I ducked behind the bushes, in an attempt to remain unseen. Footsteps sounded nearby, beating across the street pavement. I peeked through the bushes and spotted a silver Toyota parked in the road, whose engine had been left running. The driver's side door was hanging open with the keys still in the ignition. When I looked back over my shoulder, Cabel was climbing through the window again.

"Cabel!" I whispered, knowing that the men must have broken into the basement by now. "Cabel!" I quietly yelled, terror lancing through me, as he stepped inside.

No matter how much my ankle hurt, I couldn't watch Cabel blindly lead himself into the lion's den. Scared for his life, I pushed the pain out of my mind and moved close enough for him to hear me. "Cabel!"

He turned around and stalked towards the window, his face etched with concern. He had been looking for me in the empty room. "There you are," he said.

"Cabel, we have to get out of here!" I leaned against the window sill, planting my left foot in the grass.

Suddenly, the ceiling began to collapse, and one of the armed men tumbled down the staircase and into the basement. I gasped aloud, reaching for Cabel's hand through the window. But I couldn't grab him before the man on the floor fired his gun.

www.ingramcontent.com/pod-product-compliance
Lightning Source LLC
Chambersburg PA
CBHW020911200626
46814CB00001BA/274